BAD BOYES

Jim and Duncan Eldridge

Illustrated by David Mostyn

Beaver Books

Also in Beaver by Jim and Duncan Eldridge
How to Handle Grown-Ups
What Grown-Ups Say and What They Really Mean
Bogeys, Boils and Belly Buttons
More Ways to Handle Grown-Ups

And by Jim Eldridge
The Wobbly Jelly Joke Book

A Beaver Book
Published by Arrow Books Limited
62–5 Chandos Place, London WC2N 4NW

An imprint of Century Hutchinson Ltd

London Melbourne Sydney Auckland
Johannesburg and agencies throughout the world

First published 1987

Text © Jim and Duncan Eldridge 1987
Illustrations © Century Hutchinson Ltd 1987

Set in Century Schoolbook
by JH Graphics Ltd, Reading

Made and printed in Great Britain
by Anchor Brendon Ltd
Tiptree, Essex

ISBN 0 09 947200 7

Introduction

Well, it had to happen. Those of you who have read *How To Handle Grown-Ups*, *What Grown-Ups Say And What They Really Mean*, and *More Ways to Handle Grown-Ups* will have read the extracts from my diaries, 'The Diaries of X', in those books. Many people (me included) thought they were the best bits. Recently the publishers of those books approached me and asked me if I would like to write a whole book all about me and how I am the Best Dodger in the Universe.

Well I hesitated at first because I have found out that if people like me (i.e. dodgers) give away too many secrets, we are as good as telling the opposition (i.e. the grown-ups of this world) how to deal with us. But then the publishers appealed to my kind nature with two arguments:

1. They told me my book would help other young people in dealing with the problems of modern life.
2. They offered me money.

Well, the second argument touched me deeply and won me over, so here it is, a whole book.

However, we had one problem. The wonderful people at the BBC said they wanted to make a television programme about me and my book, and although it is very flattering to be A Star, it would make life difficult if I was only known as 'X'. For one thing, I could hardly do a whole television series with a paper bag over my head, bleeping out the dialogue every time someone mentioned my name. Also, what about signing autographs? People who couldn't write but only put down an 'X' would be signing my autograph, and there could be money in it. So, because of this, I have decided to reveal my true identity.

My name is Bryan Arthur Derek Boyes. I am fourteen years old and I am wonderful and stupendously clever and this is the most interesting book you will ever read in your entire life.

Right, that's all you're getting. If you want to know more about what happens, then you'll have to buy this book instead of just standing there in the bookshop reading this introduction. I know your sort, I do that as well. Clever, we dodgers, aren't we? But if you want to be even cleverer, buy this book and take it home now and read it. You won't be sorry. And if you are sorry – well, be clever – sell it to a friend for more than you paid for it.

Now, read on . . .

1

Have you ever noticed what idiots adults are? As soon as people reach the age when they can vote and can't be officially told off by their Mum and Dad, they have the thinking bit of their brain removed and replaced with a tape recorder that plays statements like 'I am older than you so I know better,' and 'I never did that when I was your age.' Parents are the worst offenders for this, but teachers come a very close second. (Parents who are also teachers are obviously in a class of their own, and therefore to be avoided at all costs.)

A practical example of this idiocy could be seen in a new teacher we had dumped on us at the start of the Spring Term. His name was Wiggis, and he was officially filling in for our regular form teacher, Perky Parrot, until Perky returned. (Perky had been taken off in an ambulance suffering from a nervous breakdown, and the betting said that he was now chewing grass in some funny farm for Loony Teachers and would never be seen again this side of the End of the World.)

Anyway, this new bloke, Wiggis, had obviously been told to watch out for me as the School's Greatest Dodger ('Keep your eye on Bryan Boyes, no teacher is safe while he is in this school!' etc), because he stormed into our classroom, and almost his opening words were: 'Which of you is Boyes?' This gave me my cue for the obvious joke: 'Half of us, sir. The rest is girls.'

He did not appreciate it and immediately put me in detention, proving (a) that he has no sense of humour, and (b) that he is a vile, nasty, vengeful pile of dog mess.

The fact that I was right to form this unbiased opinion of him was confirmed a few days later. I had turned up for school two hours late, as is my habit. (After all, once you've turned up at nine o'clock on the first day back, you know what's going to happen, so there's not much point in turning up at nine o'clock on the following days, is there?) As I walked into the classroom this Wiggis character gave me the sort of look that freezes sunshine, and then announced: 'You're late.' This at least proved he could tell the time.

'Yes, sir,' I replied. 'I would have been here earlier, but the driver of our bus collapsed at the steering wheel and we had to wait for another bus.'

Wiggis was not impressed.

'Really,' he said, with that sort of sneer teachers do so well. (I reckon they stand in the staff room and practise it in front of the mirror.)

'Yes,' I said. 'Luckily for him I am an experienced First Aider, so I was able to handle the situation until the ambulance arrived. It is very likely I will be mentioned for a Blue Peter Award by the bus company.'

I was just moving towards my desk, when Wiggis growled: 'You were also two hours late yesterday. Your excuse then was that your dog

had bitten your granny and you had to take it to the vet's to get its teeth mended.'

'Yes, sir,' I acknowledged. 'A tough old lady, my granny, sir.'

'Really,' snapped Wiggis, and now he looked really mean; the sneer was going up and down his face so quickly I thought he was going to dislocate a nostril. 'Well I am a tough old man, Boyes.'

'Old, sir? You? Never.' I smiled. (A bit of flattery never goes amiss with pompous grown-ups, in my opinion.)

'You will stay in after school,' he snarled.

To say I was shocked was an understatement. Me! Bryan Boyes, the school's arch-dodger, kept in after school! Alright, there had been that detention the first day back, but that had been insurance against being kept in again. To be kept in twice, and so soon after the first time, this was a disaster! My reputation would go downhill fast unless I did something about this madman.

I was still brooding on this point, while at the same time carving my initials on my desk, when Wiggis started speaking again, only this time his voice took on that 'Now, children, I want you all to be wonderful' tone that teachers use when they want something.

'Class 4P,' he announced, in case any of us had forgotten which class we were in, 'I have some good news.'

At this there was a general groaning. When a teacher tells a class he or she has got some 'good news', it usually means we're all going to be reduced to physical wrecks taking part in a sponsored walk, or something. Wiggis ignored the groans, and ploughed on with his spiel.

'We have a new boy starting at this school today, and we are fortunate to be having him in this class. Like any child new to any school, he will feel rather shy. I want you to make him welcome.'

Well of course at this there were smirks all round. A new boy, and a shy one at that! Everyone's natural bullying instincts came to the surface, and you could almost see people planning how they were going to write rude words on his books and steal his sandwiches. It was at that point there was a knock on the classroom door.

'Ah,' said Wiggis, 'I expect that will be him now. Come in!'

And with that the door opened, and the new 'shy boy' entered ... all thoughts of bullying vanished. It was obvious to all and sundry that even to describe him as a 'boy', let alone 'shy' was a breach of the Trade Descriptions Act. This kid looked like a brick wall on feet: six feet tall with huge hands, his knuckles grazed from where they were dragged on the ground. He looked like he ate six people for breakfast, raw. This 'kid' glared at us, and everyone shrank back in fear. (Except me, of course. Never give too much away is one of my many mottoes.)

'Welcome to Class 4P,' said Wiggis merrily. 'Class, this is Edward Slogg.'

The rest of the lesson was the usual boring stuff, Maths, and I got it all right because I copied the answers from Wiggis's answer book, that I had photocopied. After the lesson, as I was leaving the class, Bernetta Vincent came up to me. (Bernetta

9

is the nearest I've got to a friend in the school, mainly because she is nearly as good a sneak and a dodger as I am, and I therefore respect her. Most of the other kids were just complete idiots, like most of the adults.)

'Looks like Wiggis has got you where he wants you,' said Bernetta.

'The teacher hasn't been born yet who's got me,' I replied confidently.

'He put you in detention,' said Bernetta. 'Twice in one week.'

'It won't last long,' I told her. 'You'll see. I'll have him eating out of my hand. All I've got to do is find his weak point.'

'Say he hasn't got one?'

'Everybody's got one,' I replied.

At that point Edward Slogg (who we had already decided to call The Slug, although not to his face) came lumbering out of our classroom, stomped past us and tramped off down the corridor in search of someone to beat to a pulp. We could feel the whole building vibrate as he crunched along.

'What do you reckon his weak point is?' whispered Bernetta, nodding at the huge form of The Slug.

'Being mistaken for a tank,' I guessed. 'Anyway, I can't stand here, I'm off to find out what Wiggis's weak point is.'

With that I nipped off to the staff room.

(A note for dodgers: to be able to handle teachers you need to know what they are up to, and the staff room of any school is a necessary place to hang around. For some reason, teachers who are tight-lipped about every aspect of their life in the classroom will blurt out their whole life story, marriage problems, depressions, illnesses, etc to another teacher as soon as they get within fifteen metres of the staff room. So it was with Wiggis.)

I had just placed myself strategically behind a large stock cupboard near the staff-room door, when Wiggis came out of the staff room with Miss King, the domestic science teacher, and it was fairly obvious to anyone with half a brain that Wiggis was doing his best to chat her up. He was giving her the 'What a wonderfully interesting man I am' chat that all the male teachers do whenever they get near Miss King. In Wiggis's case, he was trying to impress her with his knowledge of old cars, although one look at Miss King's face should have told him that she was about as interested in old cars as she was in diving head-first into a barrel of rotten fish. Actually her same expression should have told him that she was equally uninterested in going out with Wiggis, but Wiggis must have had skin the thickness of an elephant's, because he kept plugging away, telling her all about piston sizes and all those other motoring figures that make listeners want to bang their heads against a wall and knock themselves unconscious. In this case Miss King refrained from bashing her head against a wall. However, in the middle of all this motoring garbage Wiggis let slip one interesting fact.

'What I'd really like,' he told Miss King, trying to impress her, 'is a Morgan.'

Miss King was obviously as much in the dark as I was about what a Morgan was – for all we knew it was a washing machine. Before I could discover more clues as to what constituted a Morgan, Miss King's patience finally ran out; she made some feeble excuse, like she had a class, and disappeared down the corridor. Still, I had my information as to Wiggis's weak point, and I lost no time in putting it into practice.

I waited till the crucial time, the bell for the end of school. As we were rushing out of class as if they were giving away money for the first person home, I paused just behind Wiggis, and said to my friend Weed, 'Here, did I tell you that my Dad's selling his old Morgan?'

Weed was baffled. He looked at me and opened his mouth, about to say, 'What's a Morgan?' or 'Your Dad hasn't got a Morgan,' or something equally incriminating. Fortunately I saw this coming, so I stuffed my hand over his mouth before he could get the first word out.

'Yes,' I continued. 'Amazing, isn't it? Fancy him selling it, after all this time.'

I then took my hand away from Weed's mouth (an advisable thing to do because he had gone a funny shade of purple from lack of oxygen), and hustled him out before he could put his foot in it. However, one quick look at Wiggis told me that he was hooked. His eyes and nostrils were quivering with excitement that a Morgan (whatever it was) was up for sale, and so close to hand!

My trick was working. All I had to do now was to work out what the rest of my plan was.

Later that night I sat in my home pondering on how to find out what a Morgan was. (I use the words 'my home' very loosely. Alright, I live there

with my Dad and Mum, but I have NO SAY in how it is run. I am ordered about in this house by parents who don't seem to have heard that child slavery has been abolished: 'Tidy your room,' 'Wash up,' etc. This is unfair and will change when I rule the world!)

Before I proceed with this story, I think it would be a good idea if I filled you in on the sort of parents that I have. In a word they are both crackers. Dad is just a wimp; he spends most of his evenings trying to fill in crosswords that he can't do, and just about has them half done before it's time for him to get up and go to work in the morning.

Mum is always doing something new. The day she learnt to read was a bad one for the Known Universe, because every time she goes to the library and sees a book on something she's never done before, she decides to take that thing (hang-gliding, bricklaying, walking on water, whatever) up as her latest activity. We were in a bit of a quiet spell at the moment, because the brick wall that she'd built two days before had collapsed when a dog peed against it, so she'd given up bricklaying. She was now catching up on her Open University stuff. It wasn't as much fun to watch, but at least it was quiet. (One time she was into banging an Oriental gong, and we couldn't hear for a week.)

Anyway, there we were at home, and I thought I'd try this Morgan problem on Dad. After all, anyone who does as many crosswords as he had must have heard of one.

'Dad,' I said. 'What's special about a Morgan?'

From the blank expression on his face I could see I was going to be no nearer finding my answer.

'A what?' he said.

'A Morgan,' I said. 'It's a car.'

'Oh,' he said. 'Well, er. . . .'

And then he lasped into silence while he pretended to scan what he called his memory. Fortunately for me, Mum had obviously done a course on it at some time, because she came in with, 'They're collectors' sports cars. Handbuilt. They're very rare nowadays.'

'Oh,' I said. 'Ta.'

Being Mum, however, she didn't leave it at that.

'Why?' she asked.

(Have you ever noticed that grown-ups always do that? They always want to know 'Why?' And they expect an answer. If *you* ask *them* 'Why?' they tell you to shut up and go away.)

'Oh, we're doing a project on old cars at school and someone mentioned it.'

Then, deciding it was a good idea to change the subject, I added, 'By the way, I've invited a few friends round to watch the telly on Thursday evening. There's a programme at half past eight on BMX Streetstyle.'

Notice here what a wonderful child I am, giving advance warning to my parents that I wanted to watch a particular programme on the television. This is to ensure that I won't have a lot of arguments when the time comes for the programme, and it nearly always works. However, in this case I was wrong.

'Well you can just uninvite them,' said Mum. 'I'm having a Senegalese evening here on Thursday, and that television is staying off.'

Needless to say I was shocked, too shocked to ask what on earth a Senegalese evening was.

'But you go to your bricklaying class on Thursdays,' I pointed out.

'Not this week,' said Mum. 'Sarah Patterson's just come back from the jungles of Senegal, and she's showing examples of their culture to our Third World Studies Group here. This living room will be packed with primitive works of art.'

'But this is BMX Streetstyle!' I protested.

'I couldn't care if it's the parting of the Red Sea live. That telly is staying off.'

I was stunned. What was worse, I'd fixed up a nice little earner over this TV watching business: I had invited loads of people round to watch the BMX programme on our telly, on admission payment of food and drink (e.g. packets of salt and vinegar crisps), so I stood to have a well-stocked private larder out of it.

I was just sitting brooding on this point, and wondering how to explain to everyone that the TV watching was off, when the front door chimes went. Dad says what he nearly always says when this happens: 'Are you expecting anyone?'

This is his wimpish way of wondering who should go and open the door.

'No,' said Mum. In other words, she wasn't going to open it.

'Nor am I,' said Dad. 'Go and see who it is, Bryan.'

'I'm not expecting anyone either,' I said, still fed up over the TV programme business, and not wanting to answer the door either. However, I was overruled.

'Go and see who that is,' snapped Mum.

I went, and it was lucky I did, although I didn't realize it at first.

There on the front doorstep were these two men in badly fitting suits, loonies if ever I saw them. The one with the teeth flashed a smile at me, so it was obvious they were selling something.

'Good evening,' said the other one, the one with the brain. 'We are The Children of the Flowers. We are bringing good news to the people of this area. We wonder if we might stand here and give thanks?'

'You can stand there and freeze for all I care,' I said, and slammed the door on them, because that was the sort of mood I was in.

I was just about to go back into the living room and sulk a bit more, when an idea hit me, a stroke of sheer genius!

I whipped open the door and called to the two missionaries in as loud a whisper as I could without bringing Mum and Dad out.

'Wait a minute!' I hollered hoarsely, as if I had laryngitis, and they came warily back, wondering if I was going to throw a bucket of water over them.

'I'm sorry,' I said. 'It didn't sink in at first. You say you're bringing Good News. Does that mean you're . . . saving people from evil?'

'Well, yes,' said the one with the brain, 'in a manner of speaking—'

Before he could go on and give me all the spiel, I fell to my knees at their feet.

'Hallelujah!' I said. 'My prayers have been answered!'

At first they were taken aback by this reaction (I understand that people usually set dogs or

budgerigars on them), but then I launched into my Sad Tale.

'My parents are witches!' I said. (Horrified looks on the faces of the two blokes at this.) 'They use strange carvings to carry out their witchcraft rituals. I have been trying to find a way to break them of the hold it has over them, but I had almost given up hope, until you called at this door.'

'We must pray!' shouted the one with the teeth, and the two of them dropped to their knees, and there we were, the three of us, kneeling down in my doorway as if we'd dropped something and were looking for it.

'Fear no more,' said the one with the brain. 'We will release your parents from the hold this witchcraft has over them!'

'I was hoping you'd say that,' I said. 'What are you doing this Thursday evening at about eight o'clock?'

'Thursday?' asked the one with the teeth, puzzled. 'Why, what's happening on Thursday?'

'It's a meeting of their coven,' I replied. 'They're planning a special ritual with all these primitive carvings and things. It's hideous. Please, please (and here I threw in a sob or two), save them!'

'Have no fear,' said the one with the brain. 'We of The Children of the Flowers will come here on Thursday, and we will drive out their hideous obsessions.'

With that they got up and went off down the street, gratified that their mission had been a success. I went back indoors, now looking forward to Thursday. If things went according to plan, my TV-watching food-earner was still on.

2

The next day at school I moved Phase Two of my Get-Wiggis-Eating-Out-Of-The-Palm-Of-My-Hand Scheme into operation.

Wiggis had obviously taken the bait, because at morning break he stopped me as I was going out and said, 'Excuse me, but did I hear you say yesterday that your father was selling a Morgan?'

'Oh, I'm sorry, sir,' I said in humble apology. 'I didn't mean to raise my voice in class.'

'No no,' he said. 'That's quite alright. It's just that – this is a Morgan *car*?'

'Yes,' I said. 'It's a sports car. Handbuilt. It's an old one, though, really old. 1953, I think.'

His eyes lit up. I could tell by his expression that he could almost see himself behind the steering wheel. Trying to control himself, he said, 'Actually, I might be interested in buying it. Would it be possible to meet your father?'

'I don't see why not,' I said. 'Though he's away for a couple of weeks on business. But I can write to him and tell him that you're interested.' And then I started to dangle my price in front of him. 'He might even drop the price if he knows it's for someone I know.' And with a smile I added, 'Not that I'd do this for all the teachers in this school. Some of them who I have a lot of trouble with, I'd make sure he wouldn't sell it to them however much they offered. And my father listens to me.'

I saw him swallow, and sweat started to appear on his brow. I could almost see the battle he was having with his conscience: should he be easy with me and let me get away with things in the future, or lose the car of his dreams? As always with adults, greed and ambition won. He gave me a sickly smile.

'Then it's a good thing we get on, isn't it?' he said.

'Right,' I replied.

I smiled back, and then went out to break.

Actually, to say I went out is a bit of an exaggeration. In fact, I never got there. I was just sauntering down the corridor, feeling good about having Wiggis under my thumb, when suddenly this huge hand the size of a dinner plate came out of a doorway and grabbed me by the throat. The next second I was suspended with my feet some two metres off the ground looking eye to glaring eye with The Slug.

'Give me fifty pence a week and I won't hit you,' he growled.

I had the presence of mind to crack: 'Do you take American Express?' but then he rammed his thumb up my nose, and fear of losing a nostril helped me to find the required sum of money and hand it over. With that I was returned to earth, had my foot trodden on; and then The Slug stomped off, the building shaking in his wake.

I was leaning against the nearest wall,

recovering from this sudden assault and mugging, when Weed appeared.

'He got you, too, did he?' said Weed. 'I saw it all.'

Needless to say, I was annoyed.

'If you saw it, why didn't you leap upon him and save me?' I snapped.

Actually the answer to this question was a bit obvious, because Weed is built like a tiny skeleton. Still, it's the principle of the thing, and if Weed is to call himself my friend, then he should have intervened in a do-or-die attempt, that's the way I see it. (*I* wouldn't have, but then I am more intelligent than Weed.) Weed, however, was more concerned with telling me how The Slug had used this same money-extracting technique with other kids.

'He's got nineteen people all paying him fifty pence a week so he won't beat them up. With you that makes twenty.'

Twenty people! That meant The Slug was earning ten quid a week from his protection racket. It occurred to me that perhaps he might need a business manager, and I was the obvious person. In the meantime, there was the more immediate question of me being threatened by The Slug for fifty pence a week. Something had to be done. It was then I had an idea, another stroke of genius!

'Listen,' I said, 'tell all the other kids who are under threat from The Slug to meet me round the back of the dining hall at dinner-time. I know how we can save ourselves.'

My plan was this: for a down payment of ten

pence each from the other nineteen victims of The Slug, I would guarantee to put The Slug out of action. When The Slug was out of action and his threat removed, then each person would pay me one pound.

There was a bit of a horrified reaction to this, some of the victims muttering, 'A pound!' and all that. But as I pointed out to them, they were paying fifty pence *a week* each to The Slug, whereas the pound would be a once-only payment. Also they would only have to pay it when The Slug was out of action. In my book it was a bargain and should have been seen as such by anyone with half a brain.

A couple of them wanted to know details of my plan for dealing with The Slug, but I pointed out to them that that was my secret, and if I told them then they could use it and not pay me. What they were paying me for was my brain power, and the fact that I was the greatest schemer in the school, and someone whose dodges and schemes worked. With that they all agreed to putting their safety from The Slug in my hands, and each paid me ten pence.

This gave me one pound ninety, and my protection money for The Slug for the next few weeks.

Actually the reason my plan for dealing with The Slug was so secret was because I hadn't thought of one yet; my main purpose in gathering everyone together was to get my own payments to The Slug in my pocket. After all, safety first, and charity begins at home, and all that kind of stuff. However, being a moral person, and also aware that I had to deal with The Slug for my own safety, I set my brain to work, and it was as I was eating my sandwiches in the middle of Art and Craft that The Brainwave hit me.

We have this boy in our school called Simon Spinks, and he is such a wreck and a weed and a wimp he makes the nearest jellyfish look like Rambo. Any stranger would be forgiven for wondering why he isn't regularly taken round the back of the bike sheds and beaten up by everybody, because he looks like one of nature's victims. The fact is, though, that Simon's Dad is a professional wrestler who fights under the name of the Human Mangle, or something, and can rip buses in half with his bare hands.

Anyway, two days later at lunch-time, I was sitting in our classroom eating my sandwiches, with The Slug next to me eating half a horse between two slices of bread. Suddenly The Slug spotted a note inside his lunch-box.

'What's this?' he growled, proving as I'd always suspected that he had an IQ in single figures because it was fairly obvious that it was a note.

He took it out and started to read it. Or read it as well as he could. (I had written it in very large letters in order to help him.)

' "You are an idiot," ' he read. ' "You have a face like . . ." ' The 'reading part' of his brain obviously wore out at this point, because he thrust the note halfway up my nose and said: 'What's that word?'

I looked at the note and said, 'Pig. "You have a face like a pig." '

For a minute I thought he was going to pound

me into the floorboards with one of his great fists, so I hastily added, 'I'm only reading what it says.'

He looked at me suspiciously, as if he was going to thump me anyway, just to keep in practice. Then he changed his mind (or whatever it was he kept inside his skull that passed for a mind), and read on. As he read, he became more and more annoyed. This wasn't surprising because the note told him, among other things, that his brain was thicker than pigs' muck, that his feet smelt, etc., etc.

'Who wrote this?' he yelled at last.

'Look in your lunch-box,' I suggested. 'Whoever did it may have left a clue behind.'

He peered into the dark recesses of his lunch-box, where he kept his raw meat hamburgers and stuff, and then announced that there was nothing in it apart from his food.

'Then let's look at the note,' I suggested. 'What does it tell us?'

'It tells me I've got a face like a pig.'

'Apart from that,' I said. 'It looks to me like it's been torn from the corner of an exercise book. Turn it over and see if there's a name on it.'

And lo and behold, there on the other side was written 'Simon Spinks. Class 2B.' (Surprise, surprise!)

Of course, The Slug being The Slug lost no time in deciding to take his revenge for this slur on his facial features, and hot-footed off in search of Simon Spinks (aided by my instructions that he was normally to be found by the bike sheds).

For those of a nervous disposition I will draw a veil over what The Slug did next, except to

say that he rearranged various bits of Simon Spinks in a most unsubtle and physical way.

The result? The next day, as The Slug left school to go home and terrorize his family, there waiting for him outside the school gates was something resembling a large hairy mountain. Next to this mountain was Simon Spinks, still decorated with bits of sticking plaster and bandages.

'That's the boy who did it, Dad,' said Simon, pointing his finger at The Slug.

'Is it?' said the mountain.

And the next second, Thump! Biff! Pow! Wallop! Thump! Crunch! and The Slug was lying on the pavement blowing teeth out of his nose before falling unconscious. It was the most exciting thing to happen outside our school gates since the caretakers' strike, when an angry parent threw a bowl of soup over our caretaker.

All in all, a very successful exercise, and one that should have been worth every penny to The Slug's victims. After all, at the bargain price of a pound each they had been freed by wonderful me from The Slug's tyranny. At least, that was what they thought. However I had a little scheme up my sleeve that I intended would bring me in more than just a measly nineteen quid. I was after making Big Money. And if you read the next chapter, you'll find out just what that plan was.

3

Caught you! You thought that as soon as you started reading this chapter you would find out what my plan regarding The Slug was, didn't you? Well you will, I promise you (and being a very moral and honest sort of person, I always – well, nearly always – keep my promises).

However, first I want to tell you what happened about my Mum's Senegalese evening.

For those of you who have forgotten, or skipped reading it the first time, I had invited a bunch of friends round to watch a programme on BMX Streetstyle on our television. Unfortunately there was a double booking, because my Mum had invited her Third World Studies Group round to hear her friend Sarah Patterson tell them all about her recent exploits in the Senegalese jungle. I have met this woman Sarah Patterson on more than one occasion, and, believe me, she is boring boring boring. Frankly if it was a choice between spending an evening listening to Sarah Patterson talk about anything, and banging my head against a brick wall, I'd choose the brick wall as being the more entertaining of the two. This night she was on form as usual, holding a lump of wood that looked like Mr

Wiggis, and intoning, 'Now this is a very fascinating piece of Senegalese sculpture. Note particularly the impression created by the knees. These are hunting knees.'

Instead of her audience (which consisted of my Mum, my Dad, and three weird-looking people I'd never seen before) falling about with laughter at this, they all nodded solemnly as if they understood what she was talking about. Once again it proved to me how stupid and gullible grown-ups are. Show them a scrap of paper and tell them it's either a piece of history or a work of art and they go all ga-ga over it. Yet if I drop an absolutely identical scrap of paper on the floor they have a nervous breakdown over it and I get huge lectures on tidiness and litter.

Anyway, there was Sarah Patterson, in full flood on the subject of this amazingly uninteresting lump of wood, with all those idiots nodding in agreement with the complete rubbish she was talking, when our front door chimes went.

I checked my watch. Eight o'clock. If I was lucky, it was The Children of the Flowers on time, come to bust up the Sarah Patterson Appreciation Society, and then I could get down to some sensible TV watching. If it wasn't, then I was going to have some serious explaining to do to my friends when they arrived.

'I'll go,' offered Dad, and nipped off to open the front door. My guess was he was using it as a way out of listening to more lectures on bits of wood.

'Talking of hunting,' said Sarah Patterson

30

(which no one had been, unless you counted the knees), 'while I was in Senegal I recorded a jungle hunting call, which I thought you might all be interested in hearing.'

With that she switched on her cassette machine, and this really bizarre wailing moaned around the living room. She couldn't have timed it better. As if on cue the living room door burst open, and in rushed the two missionaries from The Children of the Flowers with about four of their mates, all clutching the biggest bunches of flowers I had ever seen. Dad stumbled after them in a sort of astonished trance, wondering what on earth was going on. Mum and Sarah Patterson and the three weirdos were equally puzzled, because it was obvious from the missionaries' wild-eyed stares that they hadn't come for a lecture on Senegal woodcraft.

'Yes?' said Mum.

'The Children of the Flowers will triumph!' yelled the missionary with the biggest bunch of flowers. 'Destroy the instruments of witchcraft!'

The next second the missionaries started grabbing hold of the souvenirs of Senegal that Sarah Patterson and Mum had placed all over the room, and started jumping up and down on them. This was too much for Sarah Patterson. She dived in, swinging punches left, right and centre with a speed that would have impressed Frank Bruno. Mum also moved in to the attack. Dad did what any intelligent person would have done in the same circumstances – he cowered in a corner. However it didn't do him much good because two of the missionaries grabbed him and started shaking him, looking for black cats and cockerels and such things.

While all this was going on I crawled unseen to the phone and put in a 999 call to report a disturbance in our house.

In ten minutes it was all over: the police had arrived, acting like the SAS, kicking in the door and jumping on everyone, and then dragging them out to a fleet of waiting police vans covered in riot gear. It was wonderful stuff, just like on the TV, and must have given the neighbours something to gossip about until the earth freezes. No sooner had the last riot van driven off, with the missionaries buried beneath all their flowers and about twenty police officers in full riot gear, than the guys from school arrived, complete with the necessary crisps, cans of coke, etc. Needless to say, they were a bit taken aback by the state of our house, which seemed to be piled high with broken furniture, bits of Senegalese culture, and bunches of trampled flowers.

'Excuse the mess,' I said. 'Mum had a few friends in.'

'Ah,' they all said, understandingly. They all know what an odd sort of woman my Mum is.

With that we sat down to watch the TV. Teeth sinking into the crisps, we waited with expectation. This was going to be THE programme.

But then . . . shock, horror! Instead of the credits for 'BMX Streetstyle', one of those idiot announcers appeared, gave a sickening smile and said: 'We regret that owing to circumstances beyond our control, we are unable to show our

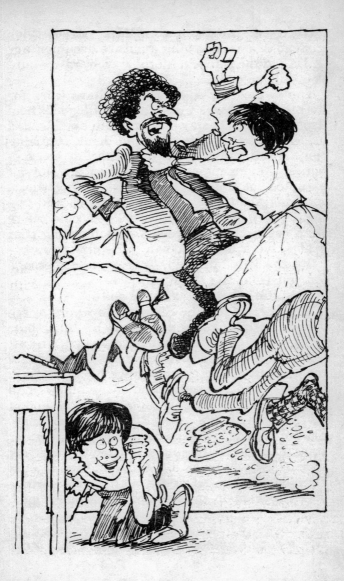

advertised programme, 'BMX Streetstyle'. Instead, we are showing a nature documentary 'A Day in the Life of a Moth', which we are sure you will enjoy.'

The swines! I ask you, all my hard work for nothing! What was worse, all my alleged school friends refused to stay and watch it, and insisted on taking back their food and drink contributions. I tell you there is no loyalty or sense of honesty among many young people today (myself excepted, of course). I was just sitting there, seething about their unfair attitudes and trying to eat as many of their crisps as I could before they noticed, when Weed said something that sent shivers up and down my spine.

'By the way,' he said, 'there was a message for you from the hospital.'

'Hospital?' I said. 'What hospital?'

'The one where The Slug is. He wants to see you. Something about the note in his lunch-box. I hope for your sake you haven't upset him.'

Aaaargh! ! ! ! Had he found out it was really me who put the note in his lunch-box? If he had, not only did it mean the end of the plans I had in mind for The Slug, it could mean the end of me, full stop. Bryan Boyes, RIP, Ripped In Pieces. Should I leave the country immediately, or should I call on him and see if I could talk my way out of whatever it was he had found out? I decided to call. After all, nothing too serious ought to happen to me in a hospital, I hoped.

The next day I visited The Slug in the hospital. Whatever he wanted to say to me, I was quite relieved to see him strung up in traction like Kermit the Frog having a rest.

'Hello,' I said. 'I hear you wanted a word with me.'

'Yes,' he growled. 'I want you to find out who it really was that put that note in my lunch-box.'

'But I thought you'd found out,' I said. 'Wasn't it Simon Spinks?'

'No it wasn't,' said The Slug. 'I was set up. Someone wanted to get me into trouble and make me end up like this.'

I was suitably shocked and horrified.

'No!' I said. 'What a terrible thing to do.'

'When I find out who it was,' continued The Slug, 'I'm gonna tear their head off. I'm gonna thump their head right down through their body. I'm gonna punch their head so hard it's gonna look like a turnip.'

'Is this all the same head?' I asked, because it seemed to me a lot of punishment to inflict all on one head.

The Slug glared at me, and again I was glad he was tied up with bits of wire and other medical things.

'Anyway,' I said quickly, 'I wouldn't if I were you.'

'Why not?' demanded The Slug, all aggressive.

'You know,' I said. 'Your illness.'

'What illness?' he said. 'I just got hurt.'

'You mean they haven't told you?' I said.

'Told me what?'

'Nothing,' I said, making sure he could tell I was lying.

Mind, The Slug is so thick it took a lot of really

unsubtle acting. I had to roll my eyes and virtually do the death scene from 'Hamlet' before he realized something was up.

'Something's wrong,' he said at last, after a thought had finally penetrated the brick wall round his brain. (I always imagine The Slug's brain to be in some sort of orbit around the inside of his skull, with the odd thought in pursuit of it, like a lost satellite.) 'You tell me what's wrong, or I'll hit you.'

'Alright,' I said. 'You've forced it out of me, but I didn't want to be the one to tell you.'

In broken sentences (real John Gielgud stuff) I then let him force it out of me what I'd heard, that the hospital had discovered that The Slug had a fatal illness called Penguin's Disease, and sudden violent actions (such as thumping people, or thinking) could well bring on a fatal attack.

The Slug looked sick with fear.

'Are you sure?' he croaked.

'Of course,' I said. 'Haven't you noticed how the doctors and nurses look at you, trying to pretend everything's alright? Ask them. If they say something like "Don't be silly," that's their way of covering up the fact that you're going to die.'

Just at that moment the Ward Sister passed by and The Slug called out to her: 'Nurse [which annoyed her], am I going to die?' To which she snapped back: 'Don't be silly.'

That was it. The Slug's mouth dropped open in horror and he sagged back on the pillows, suddenly going all grey.

'Don't worry,' I said. 'I won't tell anyone.'

36

'But shouldn't they be told?' he asked, a sorrowful look in his eyes, obviously hoping for a collection.

'No, no,' I said. 'Once they find out that you can't hit people, they'll all start getting their own back and beating you up. For your sake, we've got to keep it a secret.'

'Right,' he said, as the awful idea of himself being on the end of a fist the size of a melon entered his pea-sized brain.

'And I won't charge much,' I said.

'Charge?' he said, puzzled.

'For not telling people,' I said. 'In fact, if we keep it really secret, you can still go on charging everybody 50p a week protection money. After all, the others are still scared because they don't know you can't hit them.'

'That's true,' he said, brightening up.

'And I'll only take 90 per cent,' I added.

'90 per cent?' he said.

'That's right. 45 of every 50p goes to me. You get to keep 5p, which is pretty generous. I could stop your racket altogether.'

'But—' he began.

'And to make it even easier, I'll collect the money for you.'

He was nearly in tears now.

'But—' he began again.

'No need to thank me,' I said. 'After all, that's what friends are for.'

And with that I ate his last grape, and went.

The next day I moved the new protection operation at school into full swing. I told the other victims that I'd been to see The Slug in hospital, and he was vowing vengeance on them all for the beating he'd suffered at the hands of Mr Spinks. I told them that I had pleaded with him, but he'd threatened to beat me with his plastered arm, and now wanted me to collect the 50 pences from each of them on his behalf. I had tried to stop him, but I had failed. Because of this I was therefore giving them each back their ten pences.

They were all a bit taken aback at me actually giving people money back, but they all felt it showed that I had genuinely tried to stop The Slug persecuting them, even if I had failed.

They all then gave me their 50 pences to give to The Slug, which meant £9 to me and £1 to The Slug.

Actually, on thinking about it, it occurred to me I didn't really need The Slug, so I didn't really need to pay him, and if he interfered with my scheme all I had to do was to threaten to punch him on the nose, and frighten him off with the thought of 'sudden death'. However, I am nothing if not kind and considerate, and after all he had suffered, maybe I ought to throw the odd penny his way.

All in all, I felt that life was pretty rosy, with The Slug under my control, with Wiggis in the palm of my hand, and now everyone else where I wanted them by using the threat of The Slug. I was doing brilliantly. I shouldn't have been so confident if I had known that doom gloom horror and disaster was just around the corner for me. Everything was about to come tumbling down around my ears.

4

The problem was that I upset Weed. Actually that was only one of the problems, although I think that the historic moment when the collapse of all my plans really began was in a Maths lesson our class was having with Wiggis.

Wiggis was giving Weed a really hard time, bellowing at him about the homework that he still hadn't handed in.

'This is the second time you have not handed in your homework, Weedon,' he stormed, giving his impersonation of Adolf Hitler. 'You have had more than enough warnings. You will do detention tonight.'

Poor old Weed started to protest, but just got shouted down by Wiggis, so in desperation he tried to use me as his excuse.

'Boyes never hands in his homework, sir,' he complained. 'He hasn't handed any to you for a whole week, and you never do anything to him.'

This, of course, was perfectly true, because I had Wiggis in my power over this alleged antique Morgan car, but Weed didn't know that. Weed's accusation had certainly put Wiggis on the spot, though, and if I was to continue having him in my power I needed to come to his aid, so I chipped in with: 'If you remember, sir, our cat was sick on my last homework and my Mum said it smelt too badly to bring it in.'

Relieved, Wiggis barked at Weed: 'Exactly. See, Weedon? It is hardly Boyes's fault that his cat is ill.'

I gave a little smile of relief to myself, but from the look on Weed's face I realized that he interpreted it as a sneer against him, and I thought for one awful moment that he was going to start asking awkward questions as to why Wiggis was being so soft on me. Luckily for me the bell went at that moment, Wiggis dismissed us, and we all filed out.

As I was passing Wiggis's desk, he called me over and started asking about the Morgan car.

'Have you – er – heard from your father yet about his – er – Morgan?' he said, all very hesitant, not wanting to upset me by appearing too pushy.

'Yes,' I replied. 'I spoke to him about you wanting to buy it, and he says that's fine.'

Wiggis nearly went into a dance routine of ecstasy there and then.

'Excellent!' he breathed, and his eyes sort of misted over with happiness.

'That's what I thought, sir,' I smiled sweetly. 'He said he'll talk to you about it as soon as he gets back from his business trip.'

And with that I trotted off to my next class.

That would have been that, and everything in the garden would have been fine, if my Dad hadn't chosen that day to call in at the school and pick up some posters for the PTA. My source for what happened next comes from my friend Bernetta, who spends most of her school day hanging around the staff room or underneath teachers' cars so that she can find out what they're up to. Bernetta Vincent is the nearest thing to the Perfect Spy, and if the Russians or the Americans ever find out just how good she is they will get rid of all their own spies and try to hire her instead, because at eavesdropping she is superb.

According to Bernetta, Wiggis was walking with Miss King along the corridor near the Headmaster's office, still trying unsuccessfully to chat her up, when he heard the Head call out, 'Thank you for coming in, Mr Boyes!'

Apparently Wiggis's head turned so fast it nearly unscrewed from his neck, and he hotfooted after my Dad (with Bernetta in skilful shadowy pursuit), and their conversation went like this:

Wiggis: 'Has your son mentioned anything to you about a Morgan?'

Dad: (baffled) 'What Morgan?'

Wiggis: 'Your Morgan.'

Dad: 'No, I'm Boyes.'

Wiggis: 'Yes, I know.'

Dad: 'Are you feeling alright? I know there's a lot of strain in the teaching profession, Mr . . . er . . . What is your name again?'

Wiggis: 'Wiggis.'

Dad: 'Not Morgan?'

Wiggis: 'No. This Morgan's a car. Yours. 1953.'

Dad: 'I haven't got a 1953 car of any sort.'

Wiggis: 'But hasn't your son spoken to you about it?'

Dad: 'My son?'

It was at this point that the penny dropped with both of them, and they suddenly realized that they'd been had. Fortunately for me Bernetta saw the signs and rushed off to find me and tell me before Wiggis and my Dad found me first. As soon as I had this awful news from Bernetta I did what any sensible person would do in the same circumstances, I picked up my stuff and ran out of school as fast as I could.

There was, of course, the problem of facing Dad when I got home. I solved that one by going to a police station and telling them I'd lost my memory and I didn't know who I was. They immediately took pity on this poor little lost boy, and by clever police work they found out who I was. (They looked inside my wallet and found my name and address, but it took a good ten minutes of prompting by me before they decided on this course of action. Honestly, no wonder the crime rate is so high! The coppers who dealt with me couldn't find a pair of shoes if they were nailed to the floor.)

The police sent for my parents, and when Dad and Mum arrived I just stared blankly at them and said, 'Do I know you? You look like nice people.'

Personally, I don't think Mum and Dad were convinced (certainly Mum wasn't), but at that stage there wasn't a lot they could do to prove that I hadn't really lost my memory, so I was in the clear.

The real problem, I knew, was going to be next day at school when I had to face Wiggis again. However, I was prepared for him, and I made sure that whenever I came into contact with Wiggis I was hanging around near the Head's office.

As I expected, this was a necessary course of action, because finally Wiggis cracked and started in on me with, 'What about this Morgan then, Boyes?' in a very menacing manner.

I looked back at him, puzzled, and said, 'What Morgan, Mr Wiggis? I'm afraid I don't know what you're talking about. My mind is a complete blank.'

Then out of the corner of my eye I saw the Head approaching his office along the corridor. I put my hand to my forehead, started to sway, and sobbed loudly, 'I'm sorry sir! I wish I could remember, but I can't! I just can't!'

By this time the Head had reached us, and I heard him mumble to Wiggis, 'Go easy on him. The boy's had a hard time of it. Treat him with lots of sympathy and care.'

To this suggestion Wiggis just sort of snorted and stumped off, kicking the wall as he went, muttering under his breath, and looking very unsympathetic and uncaring.

The Head then patted me gently on the head and said, 'There there. If anyone troubles you, you just come and tell me.' Then he went off to tell everyone how kind and considerate he'd been towards me.

One problem with our Headmaster is this Kind and Caring attitude of his, because it means that he will insist on poking his nose in where he shouldn't. In this case my dodge at using the Head to keep Wiggis off my back nearly backfired, because he decided that poor Bryan Boyes was in a Psychologically Disturbed and Distressed State (due to my losing my memory), so he contacted my parents behind my back and fixed up an appointment for me the very next day with Dr Robbins, the Child Psychologist!

This could have been very serious indeed for any dodger with less experience than myself. Some of these Child Psychologists are very shrewd people and therefore a great threat to us dodgers. Fortunately for me I am the Best Dodger of All, so any Child Psychologist is a piece of cake. Dr Robbins turned out to be an even easier piece of cake, because she was young and concerned and Believed In Me. All this pointed to her being a complete idiot, and fortunately for me she was.

Her consulting room, to which I was dragged by my Mum and Dad the next day, was just like the ones that psychiatrists on the telly have: all expensive modern furniture and soft lights and things. It only proves that these people who pretend to look into minds must make a fortune out of it. Perhaps they are even better at being con-artists than anyone else.

Anyway, she moved straight into action by announcing that we were going to start with some word association.

'Do you understand what that is?' she asked.

Well of course I did because we did it at my Lower School, but I wasn't going to tell her that, because I'd just hit on a way to use it to have some fun.

'No,' I said innocently, and let her explain it to me.

'I say a word,' she said, 'and what I want you to do is say the first word that comes into your head.' Here she gave me a reassuring smile. 'It's nothing to worry about, it's to give me an idea of the sort of person you are. Okay?'

I nodded. She picked up her pencil and got all ready, and said: Right—'

'Left,' I came back with, very quickly, which rattled her, as I expected it to. I knew that she had only been saying 'right' to ease herself into the conversation, which is a thing that nearly all grown-ups do.

'Pardon?' she said, which I countered with: 'Sorry.'

'No—' she began.

'Yes.'

'Stop—'

'Go.'

By now she was getting desperate and she burst out, 'We haven't started yet!'

'Oh,' I said, all wide-eyed innocent apology. 'I'm sorry.'

'That's alright,' she said, although I could tell by the way her hand now shook slightly as she held her pencil that it wasn't really alright. She gave me an intense sort of look, as if she was trying to read the lettering on the wall behind me through my head, and announced, 'Mother.'

I looked around, puzzled.

'Where?' I said.

'No no,' said Dr Robbins, a note of hysteria now creeping into her voice. 'That's the first word.'

'Ah,' I said. 'We've started.'

'Yes.'

And then I started in on the attack again, with a quick, 'No.'

That did it.

'No—!' she yelled desperately.

'Yes.' I came back with.

'Stop!'

'Go.'

'Wait—!'

'Heavy.'

'Please—!'

'Thank you.'

This last was too much for her. Now near to a nervous breakdown, she yelled out, 'Stop!'

'You've already said that one,' I pointed out.

'We haven't started yet!' She howled.

'But you said we had.'

'We had, but then we stopped,' said Dr Robbins, now obviously in need of a psychologist herself from the way she was shaking. In fact she looked like a nervous jelly. 'Look,' she said, 'I'll give you a signal to show that we've started. Alright?'

'What sort of signal?' I asked.

'I'll point to you.'

'What sort of pointing?'

'Like this,' she said, and she pointed her pencil at me. 'Okay?'

And so we were off again.

'Yes.' I snapped back quickly.

'Now—' she said, preparing her pencil again.

'Then.'

'What?' she said, puzzled.

'Electricity.'

'Electricity?' she repeated, baffled.

'Light bulb,' I said, and the penny dropped with her. This time I thought she was going to cry with the sheer frustration of it all.

'No no no no no!' she almost sobbed. 'We haven't started yet!'

'But you pointed at me,' I protested (very fairly, I thought).

'I was only showing you how I was *going* to point at you,' she moaned. At this point she obviously gave up the whole idea of word association as a bad job, because she changed her tack and attacked my psychology from a new direction. 'Tell me about this loss of memory,' she said.

I was ready for her.

'What loss of memory?' I asked.

'You lost your memory,' she said.

'Did I?' I said blankly. 'I'd forgotten about that.'

This finished her off completely. Without another word she got up, went to her door, opened it, and pointed her finger for me to leave, admitting defeat.

Game, set and match to me.

I must admit I was feeling pretty smug after the way I'd handled both my exposure over the Morgan car, and then Dr Robbins. In fact I was feeling really proud about the whole thing, and thinking to myself that if they ever gave a Nobel

Prize for Dodging I would win it hands down every year. I should have borne in mind what all these really ancient people like my Granny are always saying about pride coming before a fall.

The next day at school my fall started. I bumped into Weed in the corridor. Well, to be more truthful, he bumped into me.

'Ah,' he said. 'Just the person I'm looking for.'

I didn't like the way he said it. An edge to his voice told me that Something Was Wrong.

'I went to see The Slug in hospital yesterday,' he said grimly, and at that moment I knew I was sunk. However, no good dodger worth their salt goes down without a fight.

'The Slug?' I said. 'I'm sorry, should I know someone of that name? I'm afraid I've still got this loss of memory. . . .'

'I'll give you loss of memory,' snarled Weed, and he actually grabbed hold of me as if he meant to do me serious damage.

Luckily for me, at that moment Miss King came out of her classroom and started walking along the corridor. I managed to free myself from Weed's grip with a quick, 'Ah, there's Miss King. I've been waiting to see her.'

The next second I was in step with a surprised Miss King, while all Weed could do was glare at me and gnash and grind his teeth.

'Yes?' said Miss King, startled to find me bobbing up and down at her side like Zebedee from 'Magic Roundabout'.

Thinking quickly, I said, 'I wanted to ask you about William the Conqueror.'

'But I teach Domestic Science,' she pointed out.

'Yes,' I said. 'What was he like at cooking?'

By then we'd reached the door out to the school yard, so I was able to make my escape, but it had been a close thing.

I was just leaning against a wall, thinking that I had better avoid Weed for the next few days until he calmed down, when Bernetta appeared, back from one of her eavesdropping visits.

'Hello,' she said. 'Have you heard?'

'Heard what?' I said. 'I don't know anything. I've lost my memory.'

'About The Slug,' said Bernetta. 'Weed went to see him in hospital yesterday.'

'I know,' I said. 'Weed nearly caught me a few minutes ago.'

'You're going to have to go into hiding,' advised Bernetta.

I scoffed, or as close as I could get to scoffing under the circumstances.

'Hide?' I said airily. 'I'm not frightened of Weed.'

'I'm not talking about Weed,' said Bernetta. 'I'm talking about The Slug.'

Once more I felt a cold sensation crawl up my spine, and the hairs on my head stood up.

'The Slug?' I said.

'Yes,' said Bernetta. 'When Weed went to visit him yesterday The Slug told him what you'd said about him having Penguin's Disease, and Weed told him you'd made it all up.'

'What?' I said, aghast, visions of me being beaten into porridge by The Slug now seriously looming up in my brain.

'And Weed told him it was you who put that

51

letter in his lunch-box, pretending it was from Simon Spinks.'

At this I was shocked. More than shocked, I was devastated. Was there no loyalty any more?

'How do you know?' I asked, hoping desperately that none of this was true.

'My sister's a nurse at the hospital,' said Bernetta. 'She overheard Weed and The Slug talking yesterday.'

Proving that this eavesdropping was a family tradition among the Vincent clan.

'Anyway,' I said, 'at least I'm safe for the present. When I last saw The Slug he was hanging from the hospital ceiling like one of these string puppets. At least he won't be free to hunt me down for a while.'

'That's where you're wrong,' said Bernetta. 'They diagnosed him wrong at the hospital and put the wrong label on him. They thought he was a bloke who'd fallen off a lorry. My sister says it happens all the time.'

This revelation was the final destruction of my illusions. If we cannot depend on the medical profession to keep people safely bandaged up in hospitals, then who can we trust? My whole world was fast collapsing about my ears.

'So what's happening to him?' I asked. 'How long are they going to keep him in?'

'They aren't,' said Bernetta. 'He came out of hospital today. He's coming back to school tomorrow.'

5

The next day I did what any other sensible person would have done in my terrible situation: I pretended I was ill and stayed at home in bed. I decided that some rare form of flu was the best thing to go down with, so I worked hard on Mum. When she came to take my temperature I stuck the thermometer against the radiator while her back was turned, and I made my eyes red by rubbing them. With Dad it would have meant an easy week off. But Mum, who is much more suspicious of me for some reason, bore with this for just two days, then called in Dr O'Rourke, our family doctor, who had the nerve to tell her that I was perfectly fit and there was no real reason why I shouldn't go back to school! The swine! The unfeeling brute! In my opinion the man is not fit to be a doctor. I immediately wrote an anonymous letter to the British Medical Association saying that he ought to be unfrocked, or struck off, or whatever it is they do with rotten doctors, in the hope that his decision to return me to school would then be null and void. I told them that Dr O'Rourke wouldn't recognize a germ if it came up and punched him on the nose, that he was the sort of doctor who cut off the wrong leg in operations, and that if he examined a dead body he would say it was perfectly fit.

However, the damage had been done as far as I was concerned, with Mum insisting that I go back to school.

During my three days off school 'ill', Bernetta had popped in now and then to give me an update on The Slug's activities, just in case he decided to come and get me in my house. According to her he spent every spare minute of his school day hanging around the school's front gate, waiting for me to reappear so that he could turn me into dog food. With that being the case it obviously would have been sheer suicide for me actually to go back to school, so the next day I took my lunch from Mum, set off for school, and instead went to the park and spent the day annoying the park attendants. I also drew up a list of places where I could spend the next few months without going to school: shopping centres, even museums and art galleries (no one would ever think of looking for me there!).

Unfortunately I reckoned without Fate and Coincidence and Bad Luck, which had all been plaguing me lately. It was just my luck that my Dad bumped into Wiggis in the town. Of course Wiggis asked him how I was because I hadn't been at school for so long. The result of this was that Mum said she was taking no more chances, and that she would take me to school herself the next day. In other words my goose was well and truly caught, plucked and cooked, and so would I be as soon as I got inside the school gates.

It was with heavy heart, and my brain

wondering if I could get a good cheap life assurance policy before we actually reached the school gates, that we set off the next morning, Mum driving and me tied up in the back, unable to escape.

'I'm too ill to go to school,' I complained.

'I don't care if you've got a combination of the Black Death and the Plague, you're going to school.'

So much for caring parents!

'I shall report this to Amnesty International!' I warned her, but it was all to no avail.

'You're going to school and that's final,' she snapped.

What was worse, she insisted on waiting in the car outside the main entrance to the school until I had actually gone in. It was terrible, especially with the sight of The Slug pacing around just inside the gates, a look of glee on his face as he saw me, like a hungry shark spotting a sailor adrift on a raft.

Oh well, I thought, if I'm going to get beaten into marmalade I might as well do it with Mum as a witness. That'll make her feel guilty. And with that I crept towards the school gates. I was nearly there when – Oh Praise Be! Glory Hallelujah! – Miss King appeared, walking towards the school gates and carrying her briefcase. With a speed that would have impressed Sebastian Coe, I hurtled towards her, and snatched her briefcase from her fingers, saying, 'Please, Miss King, let me carry that heavy bag for you.' Before she had time to protest I was walking beside her. Actually 'walking beside her'

doesn't really describe it properly, I was walking so close to her that I was almost stuck to her. It was in this way that I was able to get through the school gates past The Slug without him pummelling me through the concrete. All he could do was grind his teeth, much as Weed had done a few days earlier. In this way I got into the school building.

I won't go into detail here to describe that awful first day back, except to say that I spent most of it hiding in the school boiler house, and by the time the final bell went for the end of school I was already halfway towards my house. Day One over, and somehow I was still alive. The question was, how long could I keep it up?

Mum was as unsympathetic as ever when I got home.

'They said I looked ill when I got to school,' I said. 'They said I should have stayed at home.'

I might as well have been talking to a brick wall, all her attention was on her latest hobby: making boots out of bits of leather. As I've said before, my Mum has this obsession with finding a new interest every few weeks. None of the furniture in our house is any good because she has either (a) re-painted it; (b) made it; (c) recovered it; or (d) anything else that results in it looking like it's been dropped from a great height. Her new thing was boot-making. She finished bashing a bit of leather into some odd shape, and then suddenly said, 'Mrs Worple was asking after you today.'

'Why?' I said hopefully. 'Does she think I look ill?'

'She wants your help.'

Immediately I was suspicious. As soon as any grown-up asks for your help you know that it must be something terrible, because it's either something so hideous that no grown-up would want to do it, or so big that it would be too expensive for them to hire any grown-up to do.

'What at?' I asked cautiously.

'She and Mr Worple are going away on holiday next week. They want you to look after their pets while they're away.'

'Never,' I said, 'I'd rather drown in cold porridge.'

'I said you'd love to,' said Mum, ignoring my wishes completely.

'But I hate their pets,' I protested. 'Their cats spit at me. And even their goldfish glares at me.'

'She said she'd pay you.'

Isn't it amazing how people can nearly always find someone's soft spot?

'Alright,' I conceded, 'it sounds a good idea. When do I start?'

'She wants you to go round and she'll show you where everything is,' said Mum, now hammering away at another poor piece of leather.

'I know where everything is,' I pointed out. 'I've fed her cats before.'

'Go round anyway,' said Mum. And with a heavy note of warning, she added, 'And I don't want you getting up to any of your tricks round there.'

I was offended. Me, of all people. Getting up to tricks! Especially when there's money involved. Some things are sacred.

'What tricks?' I demanded indignantly.

Mum ignored my direct question, which is another trick grown-ups use all the time, and instead lectured me, while still bashing her boot into shape.

'Mrs Worple is a very influential person. I'm standing for the Chair of our Third World Group, and I need her support, so I don't want you upsetting her.'

'I thought you sat in a chair, not stood for it,' I commented, but not loud enough for her to hear. After all, she was armed with a hammer and various other bits of boot-making equipment, and there are times when it pays to be sensible.

Anyway, she had arranged with the Worples that I would go round to receive my instructions from them the next evening. This assumed that I would not have been pasted all over the nearest wall by The Slug in the meantime. To make sure that this did not happen (after all, this cat-sitting for the Worples could be worth a few pounds for some fairly easy activity), I set off for school the next day as per usual, so as not to arouse Mum's suspicions, but spent the day in the park.

I took the precaution of meeting Bernetta in the park at lunch-time so I could catch up on The Slug's actions, which seemed to consist of breathing fire at the mere thought of me, and stomping around the school in search of me to kick. So far so good. So long as I continued to stay away from school I was safe, or so I thought. As things turned out that evening, I was dreadfully, hideously, horribly wrong.

I turned up at the Worples' house at half past four, as requested, and found Mr and Mrs Worple all ready and waiting with ten cat dishes laid out in a row in the living room, one dish each for food, one dish each for milk. Honestly, these cats had better living conditions than I did! Each dish had its owner's name painted on it: Poo-Poo, Tiddles, Tiger, Cocoa, and Winston. Of the cats there was no sign at all.

Mr and Mrs Worple started straight in on the whole psychology of feeding their precious cats. You and I, being mere mortals, would have assumed that it was just a simple case of opening a tin of cat food, forking it out, and Hey Presto! job done. Wrong!

'It's important to make sure that they know you love them,' simpered Mrs Worple.

'I don't have to kiss them, do I?' I asked doubtfully. You can't be too sure with these cat lovers.

'Give them a smile when you give them their food,' added Mr Worple.

'Smile,' I said, to let them know I was taking all this in. 'Right.'

'Each of them a different smile,' put in Mrs Worple.

'Right,' I said again, hoping they'd be really impressed by my attention to detail.

'And make sure they have the same amount of food each, otherwise they get jealous.'

'Right,' I said for what seemed like the umpteenth time. Then, thinking that I was getting the thin end of the dialogue, I added, 'Where are they at the moment?'

'They're waiting until you've gone,' said Mrs Worple. 'They're very sensitive.'

'Sensitive,' I said. Then, thinking the

conversation called for a return to my regular dialogue, I threw in another 'Right.'

It was at this point that I half-turned, and there, glaring in through the Worples' window directly at me, was the hideous face of The Slug! Aargh! ! ! !

For a few seconds everything went blank and I thought that I was going to pass out, but I recovered and managed to pass it off with just a bit of coughing and spluttering.

'Are you alright?' asked Mrs Worple, looking very concerned.

'Oh yes, fine,' I gasped. 'Fine. It's just this cold I've had.'

'A cold?' said Mr Worple, looking very worried. 'Oh dear, I hope you won't give it to our little ones.'

For a moment I was baffled, and started looking around for their tiny children, before I realized they were talking about their cats. I suppose fears of me leaving thousands of germs lying all over their house for their cats to tread in had them worried, because the next second Mr Worple was guiding me towards the door with a genial 'Well, Mrs Worple and I have a lot to do to prepare for our holiday, and we're sure you have to get back home.'

One look at the face of The Slug pressed against their window pane, like a malevolent cod, made me determined to stay in the safety of the Worples' house until he had gone.

'Actually,' I said, there are – er – still a few things I'm not sure about.'

This stopped them in their tracks.

'Oh?' they said.

'Yes. I think it's best if I know the complete history of your cats. I want to make sure that any tune I might accidentally whistle won't bring back any unpleasant memories from their kittenhood.'

I could see that I had the Worples baffled by this, but they decided to humour me. After all, I could have been a very caring cat-minded person, interested in cat psychology. On the other hand I could have been a genuine lunatic.

'Well, starting with Poo-Poo,' began Mrs Worple. 'We found her in our garden shed about five years ago. . . .'

And so it went on, for almost two hours. All of this time The Slug remained where he was. At one point he was getting so impatient I thought he was going to try and eat his way through the window.

Finally, as the time drew near to seven o'clock, and even the Worples had exhausted all their cat stories, they started to look at their watches in a meaningful way. However, I was determined to hang on for as long as I could.

'Going back to this rubber mouse that Tiddles played with in 1981. . . ,' I prompted, in the hope that more reminiscences would come out.

The Worples didn't pick up the hint.

'Look,' said Mr Worple, stifling a yawn, 'I know you're concerned for our little ones' welfare, and we're obviously delighted at the interest you've shown in them—'

'Delighted—' added Mrs Worple, forcing a smile and herself stifling a yawn, all at the same time, which was pretty impressive.

'But we do have things to prepare,' added Mr Worple firmly. A bit too firmly, I thought.

'Of course,' I said sweetly. 'Don't let me stop you.'

This obviously wasn't the reaction they'd hoped for. There was a pause, then Mr Worple said pointedly, 'Aren't you going?'

'Oh, yes,' I reassured him. 'I'm just on my way.'

Again there was a long pause, then Mr Worple asked, 'When?' which I thought was a bit rude.

'When what?' I asked, desperately playing for time.

'When are you going to go?'

It was no use; my time and all my excuses were up. Still, there was one chance left.

'Actually,' I said, 'would you mind if I left through your downstairs toilet window?'

To say the Worples were surprised by this request would be an understatement.

'I beg your pardon?' said Mr Worple, and from his face it was clear he was wondering whether to call the local mental hospital and find out if anyone answering my description had escaped. Mrs Worple was obviously equally worried about leaving her precious cats in the care of someone as odd as I seemed to be. Would I eat them? I could almost hear her brain thinking. I hastily came up with an explanation.

'I have this phobia about doors,' I said, that being the first thing that came to my mind.

And with that I left them standing in a baffled state, and headed for their downstairs toilet.

Unfortunately for me The Slug must have worked out what I was up to, because just as

I slipped through the window of the Worples' toilet and my feet touched the grass of their back lawn, a huge hand that seemed to consist of twenty-seven fingers, each one the size of a gigantic pork sausage, wrapped itself round my head.

'Got you!' said The Slug, finally triumphant.

I could not deny it, he had. My head felt like a bowling ball, with a thumb in my ear and one finger up each nostril. I was in a very serious spot indeed.

'Well, well,' I said, with as much pretend cheeriness as I could muster considering the circumstances, 'fancy running into you. How are you?'

The Slug ignored the social niceties.

'So! I had Penguin's Disease, did I?'

'You're looking a lot better,' I commented.

'*You* put that note in my lunch-box!'

'Me?'

His grip on my head tightened and I could feel my brain being squeezed.

'Do you know what I am going to do to you?' he demanded, with a sort of growl.

'Let me off?' I suggested hopefully.

'I am going to tear your arms off and make you eat them.'

'But I've just become a vegetarian.'

'I am going to do so much damage to you that there won't be enough of you left to put in a matchbox.'

'Are we talking about a large matchbox. . . ?'

In answer, he tightened his grip even more, and I realized that unless I did something pretty

quick I was going to end up with a head the size of a small grape.

'Alright!' I yelled. 'But before you hit me, how about a deal?'

I felt his grip loosen a little, just enough for me to be aware that my nostrils were separate from each other.

'What sort of deal?'

'A TV set?'

'Eh?' he grunted, puzzled.

'And a video recorder.'

'I don't get you,' he said, baffled.

'If you don't hit me I'll give you a TV set and a video recorder.'

His grip relaxed even more, and now I could breathe again just a little.

'What? If I don't hit you?'

'And a record player. A stereo cassette player. And a microwave oven and a food mixer.'

At this he relaxed his grip on my head, and just held my ear between his finger and thumb while he thought it over.

'Alright,' he said at last. 'But if you're trying to con me—'

'I wouldn't do that,' I reassurred him hastily.

'Alright,' he said. 'When?'

'Be at my house just after midnight,' I told him. 'I'll have the front door on the latch. And you'd better bring a barrow.'

6

That night we sat in our living room watching the television. Actually, when I say 'we', I mean that Dad was watching it. Mum was bashing the daylights out of a piece of innocent leather to make something else to do with a boot, and I was pretending to watch the telly while I brooded on my plan to escape from a terrible amount of damage at the hands of The Slug, and how I was going to carry it out.

In the middle of all this, Dad suddenly came out with one of his 'thoughts', which he does occasionally to try and impress us that he is a deep thinker. Actually these thoughts usually consist of the most obvious statement that anyone could ever make, from Rover the next door's dog upwards. Unfortunately, tonight's great brain message shifted towards a subject I would much rather have avoided, especially tonight.

'Don't you think it's amazing,' said Dad, 'the way electricity affects our lives.'

Mum was obviously baffled at this philosophical outpouring coming from Dad's arm-chair, and asked, 'Why? Did you electrocute someone at work today?'

'No,' said Dad, 'I was just thinking of all the things in this house that run on electricity. The TV. The video. The microwave. The food mixer. The stereo. Don't you think it's amazing?'

I could feel myself sinking down further and further into my chair. Of all nights, trust him to start talking about those pieces of equipment.

'We'd be at a dead loss in a power cut,' he added.

'You'd be a dead loss with a full supply of electricity,' commented Mum acidly, and turned back to attacking her bit of leather.

'What I'm saying is,' said Dad, just in case we had missed the point, 'that we have built our lives around electrical appliances. Without them we'd be lost.'

With that he sank back into a contemplative silence as he watched some basketball player do something amazing with a ball on the television. Mum waited. When nothing more was forthcoming, she said, 'Is that it?'

'What?' said Dad.

'Your thought for the day.'

'Well,' said Dad philosophically, 'you've got to admit, it's a thought.'

'Yes,' said Mum, 'I suppose it does fall into that category.'

With that she picked up another piece of leather and started to pull it into odd shapes. Dad, meanwhile, turned to me, as I had dreaded he would throughtout this scintillating conversation.

'What do you think, Bryan?' he said chattily. 'Can you imagine this house without the TV and the video, the microwave and the stereo?'

'No,' I said. I was sorely tempted to add: But when we all get up tomorrow I think we'll have a pretty good idea of what things will look like without them.

It was just after midnight when The Slug turned up with his wheelbarrow, as arranged. Mum and Dad were in bed, fast asleep, fortunately, because it took us what seemed like ages to load all the stuff on to his barrow. How he managed to wheel it away was beyond me. Once again it occurred to me that he was really the Incredible Hulk in disguise. I gave him two minutes to get halfway along our street, and then I phoned the police with an anonymous tip-off about a burglary, and a large youth seen creeping away and pushing a barrow with lots of electrical goods in it. That, I thought, should put The Slug behind bars and off my back.

Luckily, it did, although not in the way I had intended. As it turned out, the burglary (of which The Slug protested his innocence, naturally, but who would believe an obvious thug like him?) only netted him a year's probation, which I thought was outrageous. I felt he should have been chained up in the deepest dungeon they could find. What got him put behind bars was his behaviour in the juvenile court. Never one to hide his temper, he expressed his displeasure at being given a year's probation, for something he protested he hadn't done, by grabbing hold of the chief magistrate and throwing him through a window. It took seven police officers and three court ushers to overpower him. The result? Six months at a detention centre

somewhere in the middle of nowhere, proving that it's fine to burgle as many houses as you want, but chuck the odd magistrate through a window and they throw the book at you.

Anyway, at least that was The Slug out of the way, and my problems were over as far as he was concerned. At least, that's what I thought. I was wrong.

Two days after The Slug was sent away on his enforced holiday, a letter arrived for me. It never occurred to me before I opened it that it would be from The Slug, because it never occurred to me that he could write. The contents of the letter froze me to my marrow, and various other bits of me felt a bit cold with fear at the same time.

The letter read: 'You have done me wrong. I want a hundred pounds from you, or I will send my big brother round to tear your head off. Then I want a hundred pounds every month until I get out. Yours sincerely, Edward Slogg.'

Aaaaargh!!!!!

Even the very words 'BIG brother' struck fear into my soul. You had to see The Slug to believe the size of him, he was so huge, like a cross between a brick wall and a Centurion tank. The idea of him having a brother bigger than him was unthinkable! I imagined the house they lived in didn't have any doors because they would never have fitted through them. In fact I thought it was unlikely their house even had walls!

And a hundred pounds now, and a hundred pounds a month from then on! Aaaaargh!!!!

I was trapped. There was no other word for

it. But as any good dodger knows, when you are trapped is when you must be at your brilliant best. Fear of being pummelled into tiny lumps of bashed-up human being does wonders to the best dodgers' brains, and I wasn't only one of the best, I was *the* best.

Somehow, some way, I had to raise the first hundred pounds. That would buy me a month's grace before Slug the Elder turned up to remove my ears, and in that month I could come up with some way to get out of this whole mess. Also, I had to raise the hundred pounds in a way that was legal, decent, honest and truthful, otherwise I would be breaking my own code, which is: Any Idiot Can Be A Thief; It Takes Genius To Raise Money Honestly. This is not based on as high a moral principle as it sounds, it's really founded on the commonsense view that as most thieves are idiots, they get caught.

(Actually I may be slightly exaggerating when I say that I had to raise the money in a way that was legal, decent, honest and truthful. Legal was important. As for the rest, well, no one else seems to bother so why should I? And even then, if I go by their standards, even 'legal' is a bit of a luxury.)

I was still racking my brilliant brains when I arrived at the Worples' to put the food out for their cats. It was as I was forking out tinfuls of this gunge, which always reminds me of school dinners, that I had two brainwaves at once! Note, not one but TWO! Eat your heart out, Albert Einstein! Alright, so he thought up the Theory of Relativity, but what else? Just one Theory!

Huh! While I, Bryan Boyes, on this momentous occasion of feeding five horrible spoilt moggies, had two brainwaves at once! It is at times like these that I feel almost humble to have been born in the same Universe as me, and wonder whether I should leave my brain to medical science after I have departed from this earth.

The first idea came from something that had happened to me on Saturday in the shopping precinct. I had been walking through the precinct when I had been accosted by armies of people waving tins at me and asking for money. I got grabbed by Cats' Welfare, the Stop Poverty Campaign (who plan to make us all poorer by getting us to put our money into their tins), and the Arthritic Feet Day.

This was the second time it had happened; the week before it had been Stop Whales Disappearing. (I thought at first the woman said she was collecting for Stop Wales Disappearing, and I said from what I'd seen of Wales and the Welsh the sooner it disappeared the better.)

It occurred to me at that time to wonder where all these people come from? I reckon they keep them in warehouses, all locked up with a tin with a slit in it permanently stuck in their hand, and the first sign of good weather they kick them out in the street.

Even worse, as I was leaving the town centre I actually got grabbed by someone trying to sell me a plastic poppy. I'm sure Poppy Day isn't until November. Maybe they're moving it around to confuse people into paying more than once, or perhaps they're going to have two Poppy Days a year, like the Queen's Birthdays. In fact I got accosted by two separate Poppy collectors. Fortunately I was able to fend them both off with:

1. (*to the first*) 'I disapprove of your symbol because opium comes from poppies. Do you realize that you are promoting drug addiction?'

and:

2. (*to the second*) 'I lost my grandfather in the War and all our money goes into keeping up his grave, that's why I haven't any money spare to give you. But' (*and this with a tear in my eye*) 'if you could spare some money from your tin towards the upkeep of his grave. . . .'

The second collector didn't give me any money, but certainly she didn't stay around long. (Actually we lost my grandfather in Brighton, but we found him two days later in Bournemouth.)

From my experience the best method to use with charity collectors is to burst into tears and go for sympathy. If approached by Cats' Welfare, for example, burst into tears and blub, 'I had a cat once, but it got run over. This brings it all back to me.' The collector will feel too upset to ask you for money. Mind you, choose your words in relation to the charity carefully, otherwise you could end up sounding like an idiot (e.g. for the Tree Protection League: 'I had a tree once but it got run over' just doesn't ring true).

Anyway, this was my first brainwave: I would go out with a tin and collect for charity, and the charity I would be collecting for would be me! (After all, everyone keeps telling me that charity begins at home.) Simple!

My second brainwave was this: A Pets' Holiday Home, using the Worples' house! After all, I was already looking after five cats and a goldfish. It would be a piece of cake to bring in a few more animals while their owners went on holiday, and I would make money at it! Again, simple but brilliant.

The next day I put a card in our local newsagent's window, advertising The Pets' Holiday Home. ('Give Your Pets A Holiday Too. Let Them Stay At The Best Place In Town: Bryan's Pets' Holiday Home.') Mum and Dad were a bit puzzled by the number of telephone calls I was suddenly getting, and I thought they might start asking awkward questions. Fortunately for me Dad is too much of a wimp to start interfering, and Mum had developed a new interest: playing the steel drums. This meant that with the noise she made practising there was very little chance of anyone holding any kind of conversation in our house, which further stopped them asking me awkward questions.

Within two days the Pets' Holiday Home was in full swing, with the addition of two tortoises, an Alsatian dog called Rex, a chicken called Adolf, one fat gerbil (which produced seven little gerbils a few days later, thus putting up its owner's bill), and a boa constrictor. Meanwhile, in the goldfish's tank there were also now one catfish, one axolotl, and one piranha fish. (Unfortunately the goldfish disappeared two days after the piranha fish went into the tank. However, life is full of such mysteries.) This was

obviously going to be a major success; I could feel it in my bones.

All in all, with two such obviously brilliant schemes as this, not only would I be able to raise the hundred pounds I needed to stop myself being turned into soup, I could quite possibly have two schemes here which could make me rich! That was the way I saw it. Unfortunately for me, I was wrong.

7

The Pets' Holiday Home Scheme started off well enough, but by the third day I was having major problems.

Bernetta called round to the Worples' house on that third evening to see how I was getting on, and found me in what might be called a thoughtful mood. What I was thinking was, I'm really in trouble here!

'How's the Pets' Holiday Home Scheme going?' she asked, surveying the scene. She had a slightly doubtful look on her face as she looked around, because there was obviously a marked lack of animals about the house.

'To be honest,' I was forced to admit, 'I'm not sure. As you may have noticed, a lot of the animals seem to have disappeared.'

'Oh?' she said, and then added, looking about her very warily, 'Does that include the boa constrictor?'

'No, no,' I said. 'He's fast asleep behind the settee. The ones who worry me most are the Worples' cats. I hope they've just left home for a bit. I keep poking the boa constrictor, just in case, but nothing moves in it.'

'What about the piranha fish?'

'He seems happy enough, although the catfish has also disappeared. There's something funny going on in that fish tank.'

'I think maybe you had the wrong mix,' she commented. 'After all, these animals don't necessarily get on very well together in the wild.'

'Yes, but they're not in the wild,' I said. 'They're in civilization. Well, at least, they're in the Worples' house. They should act like civilized people. We don't go around eating each other.'

'Who else have you lost?' she asked.

'The chicken,' I said. 'It nipped out when I left the front door open, and when I last saw it it was heading towards Sainsburys. I hope it kept away from the Poultry Section, or it'll be in serious trouble.'

'What about the gerbils?'

'They just keep multiplying. I found another two in the straw yesterday. What with that, and Rex the Alsatian dog dropping his thoughts for the day all over the house, this is not going to be as easy as I thought.'

Similarly, the charity collecting scheme was also running into all sorts of trouble. I had seriously overestimated the generosity of people who give to charity. I thought all you had to do was cut a hole in a tin and lean against the nearest wall and people came up to you and forced pound coins into your tin. In fact the reality was very different.

On my first outing, for which I decided to pose as Save The Trees, I had fixed a label on my tin with a picture of a happy tree on it. I even had a good slogan on a piece of cardboard propped up near me: 'Be Kind to Trees, Their Bark Is Worse Than Their Bite', which I thought was brilliant. However as soon as I approached people with my tin and a friendly smile, they either pretended I was invisible, or saw me and crossed over at least two main roads and did a five-mile detour to avoid me. I almost had to fall at people's feet and sob about how trees were suffering before people coughed up, and even then they didn't exactly give generously. When I got my tin home and opened it I found the whole lot added up to just over fifty pence, plus a button and an Irish ten pence. I thought these last two 'contributions' were disgusting. Honestly, fancy cheating a charity like that! It occurred to me that some people have no moral values at all.

The second charity I set up was called The Wild Bird Support Group. I put up a small table outside the gates of our local park, selling small bags of dried bread at 25p each for people to feed the birds. A bargain, you'd think, yet hardly anybody bought one. Some people even had the nerve to walk past me into the park bringing their own dried bread with them! The axe finally fell on my Wild Bird Support Group when one bird, who was obviously feeling wilder than the rest of its mates about my scheme, dropped a huge dollop of whoopsy right on my head.

The end of my charity scheme came when I was once more in the shopping precinct, this time collecting for Help Deprived Children. After all, I reasoned, no one was more deprived than me. Certainly right at this minute The Slug's big brother wanted to deprive me of a hundred pounds, which I hadn't got.

Anyway, I was standing in the precinct with my tin and wearing suitably scruffy clothes, when this man stopped in front of me.

'Here,' he said.

Good, I thought, a punter at last, and I held out my tin towards him with a saintly, 'Thank you, sir. The Deprived Children will be very grateful.'

Instead of stuffing money in my tin, he peered at me from an uncomfortably close position, and then said, 'I recognize you. You were here two days ago.'

Aargh!

'No I wasn't,' I said.

'Yes you were. Collecting for Save the Trees.'

'That was my twin brother,' I said, thinking quickly. 'We're a very concerned family.'

Unfortunately for me this man was one of those really suspicious people who won't take No for an answer. Personally I found it all a bit upsetting. After all, if people can't trust each other, where does that leave us? The man persisted.

'It *was* you,' he insisted. 'You even had that same jumper on.'

'No no,' I came back. 'It was my brother's turn to wear it that day. We're a very poor family. We've only got one set of clothes between us.'

Alright, so it wasn't the best excuse I'd ever made up, but considering that I was trapped in a very dodgy situation and was under great stress, I thought it wasn't bad. Unfortunately the man wasn't convinced.

'I've never heard such a load of old rubbish in my life!' was the exact way he put it.

Suddenly a saviour appeared, or at least, what I took to be a saviour. From out of nowhere this vicar suddenly popped up, all back-to-front collar and smiles to bring comfort and joy to everyone. Right at that moment he seemed like an oasis in a desert. I nearly yelled out Hallelujah there and then.

'What seems to be the problem?' he asked, obviously seeing this situation as one where he could do Good Works.

'This boy here—' began the suspicious man in the sort of voice that I knew would proceed to denounce me unless I did something about it. Quickly I threw in, 'I'm collecting for the church.'

It did the trick. The vicar's face lit up as if someone had pressed a switch.

'Really?' he said.

'Yes,' I said. 'For deprived children.'

'Why, that's wonderful!' said the vicar.

I gave a modest smile, and was just thinking I'd got away with it, when his next words struck doom into my heart, and my pocket.

'By sheer coincidence I'm right at this very minute on my way to a meeting of the Deprived Children's Fundraising Committee. They'll be delighted at this gesture. Thank you so much.'

And before I could so much as make a move, he had lifted the tin out of my hand.

'But—' I began.

'No need to thank me,' beamed the vicar. 'I'm going there anyway, and it'll save you the trouble. I must say it does my heart good to see

such devotion to charity work, helping others so much less fortunate than oneself, especially when one hears so many awful things about the youth of today. Well done, my boy. Well done.'

And with that he was off through the shopping precinct with my tin. I was stunned. Theft! Robbed by a vicar! I turned to the suspicious man, appealing to him for help of some kind. Why didn't he trip the vicar up before he got away? The man did not appear at all sympathetic to me. In fact all he said was, 'Well I'm not convinced. I reckon he wasn't even a real vicar. I reckon he was your accomplice. Anyway, I know where you live and I'm going to call on your parents and complain, so don't think you're getting away with it!'

With that he went off, too, leaving me even worse off than I had been before!

That night my heart was heavy as I made my way to the Worples' to feed the menagerie. After I had been there for a few minutes, it was even heavier. The rate of disappearance of the animals seemed to have accelerated. The piranha fish seemed as happy as ever, but of the axolotl there was no sign. I remember David Attenborough saying in his 'Life on Earth' programme about how the axolotl was very rare. I guessed it was even rarer now.

The worst thing was finding the boa constrictor had disappeared from its usual place behind the settee, and was nowhere to be seen. The Worples' cats were also nowhere to be found. My Holiday Home was now reduced to a cageful of ever-increasing gerbils, Rex the Alsatian, two tortoises, and one cheerful piranha fish.

I was just standing there, thinking to myself that at least I still had two days left to work out what to do about the whole Pets' Holiday Home scheme before the Worples returned, and wondering what they would say if they walked through their front door right now, when I heard the front door open. The next second I heard Mrs Worple's voice trilling happily, 'We're home, babies!'

My heart froze.

8

Before I had a chance to make a run for it, the living room door opened, and there was Mrs Worple, closely followed by Mr Worple, complete with suitcases.

They seemed a bit taken aback to find me there, but then realized that I was officially there to feed their animals, so Mrs Worple switched on her smile and said, 'Hello, Bryan. I expect you're surprised to see us back early.'

'Yes,' I admitted, although 'shocked and horrified' would have been better words to describe my feelings.

'We couldn't stand being away from our little ones any longer,' said Mr Worple, plonking down the suitcases. 'How have they been? Have they been missing us?'

'Oh yes,' I said. 'Missing is definitely the right word.'

However Mr Worple had stopped listening to me and was wrinkling his nose in a funny manner.

'What's that smell?' he asked.

Actually it could have been one of many, from Rex the Alsatian's doggie poos dotted around the house, to the gerbils, or even the tortoises.

However, it seemed safer simply to say, 'What smell?'

Mrs Worple had also joined in the general sniffing.

'It smells like . . . mice,' she said.

'Hamsters,' said Mr Worple.

Gerbils, I nearly corrected him, but decided against it.

Suddenly, from upstairs, came the sound of Rex the Alsatian barking.

'What's that?' asked Mrs Worple.

This seemed a good time for me to go.

'Actually, I must be off—,' I began, edging towards the exit, when there was a knock at the front door.

'I wonder who that is?' said Mr Worple, and proceeded to march off to the front door to find out.

Meanwhile, Mrs Worple was saying, 'I heard a dog bark.'

'A dog?' I said.

At this point she caught sight of the gerbils' cage.

'What are they doing here?' she demanded.

Before she could insist on an answer, Mr Worple returned, closely followed by a man.

'There's a man here about a chicken called Adolf,' announced Mr Worple.

'A chicken?' said Mrs Worple, baffled.

'Good heavens,' I said, looking at my watch. 'Look at the time.'

The visitor was not to be put off.

'I've just found out that my daughter sent her pet chicken to your Pets' Holiday Home,' he said. 'I'm sure she did it with the best of intentions. . . .'

Mr and Mrs Worple looked back at him blankly.

'*Our* Pets' Holiday Home?' asked Mr Worple.

Suddenly the penny dropped for Mrs Worple.

'Bryan!' she yelled.

Fortunately for me I had managed to sneak behind the settee during the discussion about the chicken.

'He's hiding somewhere,' said Mr Worple perceptively.

Then both Mr and Mrs Worple started hunting around their living room, trying to find me. Meanwhile, the man who'd called about the chicken was looking very perplexed indeed.

'What's going on?' he demanded. 'I've just come to collect my daughter's chicken.'

It was at this point that Mr and Mrs Worple's search for me led to them peering into an alcove near their bookcase, and discovering the boa constrictor, who popped out to look at them. The screams from the Worples were incredible. I didn't wait to find out what happened next, I made a run for the door, and then was off out of the Worples' house and heading back home like a rocket.

My plan was simple. I intended to get home, pack as many things as I could into a bag, and then run away. From a personal point of view, it seemed the safest option. I had worked out that it would be safe to return home in a week or so, after all the flak had died down. I was counting on the fact that if I disappeared for a week, Mum and Dad would be so worried that when I reappeared they wouldn't go on at me.

That was my plan. Unfortunately, as with all the plans that I had come up with recently, this one failed as well.

It failed because Dad caught me just as I was about to leave the house, and he was obviously in one of his 'I must form a closer relationship with my son' moods, because he insisted on talking to me. I could just have knocked him over and run off, but that would have aroused his suspicions. It was a difficult situation for me. I wanted to get away as fast and as far as I could before the Worples arrived to complain. However, it was important that I didn't appear too eager to get away.

As I say, I was halfway towards the door, when Dad saw me.

'Ah, Bryan,' he said. 'Off out?'

Proving once again that grown-ups say the most obvious things.

'Yes,' I said. 'Swimming.'

'Swimming,' said Dad knowledgeably. 'That's good.'

'Yes,' I said, and I carried on moving towards the front door.

'Healthy,' added Dad, and at this point my heart sank, because it was obvious from his tone that he intended this as a heart-to-heart talk.

'Right,' I agreed, ignoring his tone, and preparing to make a final rush for the door.

I was too late. The next second his arm was around my shoulder and he was saying, 'Son, we don't get much chance to talk, do we?'

'No, that's true,' I agreed. 'We must talk some time.'

Dad was not to be put off.

'Bryan. . . ,' he said, with his serious face on. 'Are you happy?'

Not at this immediate moment, I thought. Aloud I said, 'Yes. Very. Well, it's been great talking to you, Dad.'

Then once more I made a move for the door. I was too late. The sound of the front door chimes heralded my doom.

Before I could stop him, Dad had opened the door. It was the Worples and the man about the chicken. Worse, also on the doorstep with them was the suspicious man from the shopping precinct. It was as if Eamonn Andrews had decided to make me the subject of 'This is Your Life', and had dug up the four people I least wanted to see in my whole life.

'Hello,' said Dad cheerily.

That was the last cheerful word spoken. The Worples and the man about the chicken immediately started in with a list of complaints as long as all our arms. And over it all the suspicious man was throwing in his two penceworth, calling Dad a rotten crook, and accusing him of putting his son up to begging for fake charities.

At this point, Mum arrived. That being the case there seemed little else for me to do except surrender. The next few hours are still a painful memory for me, an occasion that I would prefer to forget. Oh well, I thought, as I went upstairs to imprisonment in my room, at least it can't get any worse. That is where I was again so dreadfully wrong.

9

Unfortunately the repercussions from the Pets'
Holiday Home fiasco continued for quite a while.
For days afterwards pet owners were calling at
the Worples' house to collect their pets, and when
no pets were to be found, they demanded compensation. The Worples in turn sent these people
round to our house.

The end result: Dad was forking out money
to these angry people as if five pound notes were
going out of fashion. I even considered sending
a friend round to claim compensation off Dad
for a non-existent pet snake or camel or
something while he was doling out all this cash,
but I decided against it. After all, he'd had a
lot of trouble and I didn't want to take advantage of him while he was down, because basically
I am a good and kind person.

Mum particularly was upset by the whole Pets'
Holiday Homes and charity scheme incidents.
For days afterwards she would lecture me,
whether I was eating or watching television or
even sleeping.

'Do you realize the shame you have brought
on this family? Do you know what your father's
name is?'

On the first occasion she asked this, I was able to answer, 'John.'

'Your father's name is mud,' she said.

This baffled me. John Mud? I thought it was John Boyes.

'Those people you cheated hold him in contempt. He is a broken man,' and so on and so on and so on.

I tried defending myself, but it was like talking to a brick wall.

'It was all in a good cause,' I pointed out. 'No one complains when other people do things in a good cause. Bob Geldof does things for a good cause, you say he ought to be made a saint. I do things for a good cause and I get told off.'

'Bob Geldof does not fill other people's houses up with boa constrictors and piranha fish,' stormed Mum.

'It was only one piranha fish.'

'It ate up all those other people's pets.'

'It only ate a goldfish, a catfish and an axolotl. I don't see what all this fuss is about. We eat fish and no one gets annoyed about that.'

'It was Mrs Worple's pet goldfish,' raged Mum. 'It had a name. It was called Robin.'

'So if I call a piece of fried cod Fred, does that mean I can't eat it?'

This argument did not go down too well. As always I was told to shut up. What was worse, they stopped my pocket money until all the people who had lost their pets had been paid back. They also wanted me to pay Mr and Mrs Worple compensation for the damage to their house. All in all, the future did not look too bright for me.

I was discussing the situation with Bernetta the next day at school. She remarked that I did not appear too miserable considering that my whole world had collapsed about my ears.

'I can handle it,' I said. 'For one thing, I have a plan.'

'I think you ought to be careful with your plans,' said Bernetta. 'The last few all went drastically wrong.'

'Only because of unforeseen circumstances. This one cannot fail.'

'Why?' she asked. 'What are you going to do?'

'I'm going to be nice to my parents. I shall start by giving Dad a birthday present this evening.'

'Is it his birthday today?'

'No, not for another six months, but I can't wait that long before I start getting pocket money again. Mum is going to be the tough one.'

'Get her something for her hobby,' suggested Bernetta.

'Which one?' I pointed out. 'Boot-making, motorbike mechanics, you name it, she does it. Her latest is martial arts.'

'Get her something for that.'

'I suppose I could give her a brick to chop in half,' I mused. Then I had an idea. 'I've got it!' I'll get her some flowers.'

'But you haven't got any money,' pointed out Bernetta, and added quickly – rather too quickly, I thought – 'and neither have I.'

'I don't need any,' I said. 'I'll go to the cemetery and take some off a grave. So long as I remember to take the card off first. It wouldn't do for her to find a message with them that reads "Rest In Peace".'

So it was I arrived home that evening loaded down with presents. Well, not exactly loaded down, to be honest. I had wrapped up a lump of stone that I had found as a present for Dad. ('It's an Iron Age axe-head, Dad. It's very rare. It's very hard to find the right present for the perfect father, but I thought that you would appreciate the beauty of this.') I had dumped the idea of grabbing some flowers from the cemetery, mainly because there weren't any there that were suitable. All I could find there were a few wreaths, and I didn't think Mum would really appreciate that. Instead I borrowed a few from the garden at number 15 in our road. After all, they had so many I knew they wouldn't miss the odd dozen or so.

Mum was suspicious, I could tell. The way she sniffed at them cautiously, I knew she was wondering if I had poisoned them so that when she smelled them she would keel over. Dad, however, was over the moon with his present. He kept going on about how beautiful it was, and what a lovely thought, and what an unusual present.

It was in the middle of all this that the front door chimes went. Eager to prove to them what a wonderful son I was I even went and opened the door.

There on the doorstep were the two missionaries from ages ago, The Children of the Flowers.

For a moment, as they say, my past life swam before my eyes. Or, at least, the bit that involved

The Children of the Flowers and Mum's Senegalese evening. Whatever this visit was about, it wasn't to bring me Good News. However, I played innocent and just said sweetly, 'Can I help you?'

The two missionaries exchanged grim glances that did not bode well for my health, and then launched into a list of what they wanted to see me about.

'Because of you,' said the one with the brain, 'we went to jail for causing a disturbance.'

'And assaulting the police,' added the one with the teeth.

'We have only just come out of prison today.'

'We have been thrown out of our Order.'

'The Children of the Flowers,' added the one with the brain, in case I'd forgotten. 'Our lives have been ruined.'

'And it is all your fault.'

Then they came to the reason for their visit.

'We have come to take our revenge.'

There was only one thing for me to do. I put on a puzzled expression and said, 'I'm sorry, do I know you?'

At this the missionaries exchanged annoyed glances, and for a second I thought they were going to jump upon me there and then.

'Are you trying to pretend you don't remember that terrible evening?' demanded the one with the teeth.

'The witchcraft?' said the one with the brain.

'Oh, that!' I said. 'I'm sorry, I didn't realize. You want my twin brother.'

That stumped them.

'Your twin brother?' they said.

'Yes,' I replied, ashamed. 'I'm afraid he's caused us a lot of bother. If you wait here I'll go and get him.'

And with that I went in and shut the door, told Mum and Dad I had to pop along to the corner shop for something, nipped out the back door and beat a hasty retreat.

From what I can piece together, the rest of the action went like this:

Knock on door. Mum opens it, and is confronted by the two ex-missionaries, whom she recognizes at once as the people who ruined her Senegalese evening.

'You!' she yelled. 'Go away, or I shall call the police!'

'We've come to complain about your son,' said the one with the teeth.

'The one who fooled us into coming into your house that night,' said the one with the brain. 'Not his brother.'

'His brother?' said Mum.

'Yes,' replied the one with the teeth. 'We understand that they are identical twins.'

'Don't you think I'd be completely insane if there were really two exactly like him!' yelled Mum at them, and then she slammed the door shut.

At which point I think the two blokes must have realized that they'd been fooled by me, because they didn't knock at the door again but went off muttering to themselves. A right pair of idiots, if you want my opinion.

However, they didn't go far, because the next

morning as I set off for school, there they were, waiting for me halfway down our road. Luckily I saw them hiding in a doorway, so I was able to beat a hasty retreat, and double round the back streets to school, but it was a close shave.

At break-time I was telling Bernetta about them, and how I was in mortal fear from these obvious loonies, when she dropped the worst bombshell of the lot.

'The Slug's escaped,' she said, 'and he's after you.'

10

I spent the rest of the day in a stunned state. The Slug on the loose! How did he get out, that's what I wanted to know? Why wasn't he kept locked up and chained to a wall? They must have known how dangerous he was. One look at him should have been enough to tell the Detention Centre authorities that what they had in their possession was something like Jaws with clothes on.

It was obvious to me where he was heading: straight for me. He knew that I had set him up with all those pretended 'stolen goods' from our house, and a brute with the killer instinct of The Slug would obviously be hunting for me.

I checked a map to plot where his Detention Centre was, and found that it was out on the marshes of the East coast, so maybe he would fall in a marsh and drown on his way.

I considered going to the police with my map and suggesting a series of road-blocks between my house and The Slug's point of escape. If necessary a complete ring of wall-to-wall police across every road between there and me. However all the police would do would be to pat me on the head and say, 'Don't worry, son, that won't be necessary.' Hah! How would they know whether it would be necessary or not? It was alright for them, they weren't The Slug's target. If The Slug was after them there'd be Centurion tanks out on the streets and nuclear weapons being fired at everything over six feet three that moved.

I told Mum and Dad about The Slug's escape and suggested that he was after me, and that I needed proper protection. All they did was say 'Why on earth should he be after you? It was us he robbed, he might just as well be after all of us.' They also added, 'Anyway, the police will get him.' Phooey! Our police couldn't catch a cold if they were stuck in freezing water up to their necks. And meanwhile my life was in danger!

I decided there was only one answer, I would have to persuade Dad and Mum to move house, and quickly before The Slug arrived.

I had a stock of reasons ready why we should move:
1. 'No one in this area likes me.' (However, when I used it once before Mum and Dad simply said, 'The way you act, we're not surprised.')
2. 'Did you know that there was an earthquake tremor in this street last week?'
3. 'Do you realize that if you sold this house and moved to a cheaper area you'd make thousands of pounds' profit? You'd be able to buy everything you've ever wanted.'

Armed with these excuses I sat down to supper the next night, and waited for the chance to use them. It wasn't as easy as I'd hoped. Mum seemed more interested in telling Dad about a phone conversation she'd had with her mum (my dreaded granny!) earlier in the day. However, I decided to come straight out with it and see how I got on. So, as they were both feeding their faces, I said, 'Have you ever thought of moving?'

They both looked at me, puzzled.

'This isn't about this Slug boy, is it?' asked Mum. 'Because if it is—'

'No, no,' I said hastily, 'I was just thinking that if we sold this house we could move somehere cheaper and get a really big house.'

'Why should we want to move?' asked Dad.

I decided a bit of ingratiating flattery wouldn't go amiss here, so I simpered at Mum and said, 'Well I think it would be good for Mum if she had more room for all the things she likes doing. It's not fair that she doesn't have anywhere special for herself.'

It didn't go down as well as I'd hoped.

'Are you being funny?' was Mum's only answer.

'No.'

At which point she decided to ignore me, and started in about my gran. I thought the conversation was moving dangerously away from the subject of us leaving the area, so I threw in, 'I hear they're going to build a Motorway at the end of our road.'

'What?' said Dad. 'Where did you hear that?'

'I can't remember,' I said. 'But I thought you ought to know. The longer you leave it, the less you'll get for the house. I reckon we ought to move now.'

'Will you shut up about moving,' snapped Mum.

'I'm only trying to be helpful,' I said.

It was no use, Mum was still carrying on about

my gran, accompanied by lots of sighs and heavy pauses, which meant there was trouble brewing on the Gran front. Mind you, if you ask me, my gran deserves any trouble that comes her way, she is a devil in human shape, a fiend incarnate, and all other rotten phrases I can think of.

'I get the impression', said Mum, 'that she wants to stay with us for a bit.'

'What?' said Dad, aghast.

I could share his aghastness. Having Gran here would be like being in one of those horror films, with Gran as the murderous loony roaming around the house.

'I think she's lonely,' said Mum. 'She says that she doesn't have any company.'

Frankly, I could understand that; Gran is so horrible she deserves to be lonely.

Suddenly a brainwave hit me. The perfect place for me to hide out, until the police caught The Slug and put him back in chains where he belonged.

'I know!' I said.

'If you're going to start on about us moving again—' warned Mum.

'No,' I said. 'Why don't *I* keep Gran company?'

You could almost see the shock on their faces as I suggested it.

'You?' said Mum.

'Yes. I could stay with her for a few days. Help her around the house. Cheer her up.'

Mum put her hand on my forehead, and then said to Dad, 'He hasn't got a temperature.' I must say I felt insulted by this slur on my motives for doing a good deed, but I decided to ignore it.

'She'll be pleased,' I added.

At that statement I saw doubt on both their faces, but as soon as they realized that the alternative was to have Gran to stay with them for a few days, they decided to keep any doubts to themselves.

So it was that the very next day I went round to my granny's flat, with my little suitcase all packed for a few days' stay. I had decided to bunk off school while I was at my gran's, because it occurred to me that school was another place The Slug would be staking out looking for me.

Before I go any further I think it would be a good idea if I said why my granny is such a frightening person. To start with she was born about a thousand years ago, and as a child she used to frighten dinosaurs. I'm not sure if she wasn't the real reason they all vanished; I reckon they all saw her coming and headed for Outer Space. In the second place, she is TOUGH, the sort of person that bites nails in half with her bare teeth. Woe betide the mugger that tries to rob my granny, she would leave them clutching bits of themselves where they never realized they had bits. Also, she does not believe in social niceties, if she does not like someone she tells them so, and in no uncertain terms.

All in all, if Rambo was given the choice between meeting my granny face to face, or swimming in a shark-infested sea, he would take the sharks, and that would be a sensible decision on his part.

Taking all this into consideration you may wonder why I had therefore volunteered to hide out at her place. The short answer is that I

thought that Gran would only glare at me, whereas I knew that The Slug would tear me limb from limb.

My arrival at Gran's was par for the course.

'What do you want?' she demanded when she opened the door.

'I'm here to keep you company for a few days,' I told her, throwing in a cheerful smile.

'Why?' she growled suspiciously.

'Because I want to help you. We've got a week off school.'

And with that I was just walking in, looking all helpful, when Gran shoved her leg across my path.

'Not yet you don't,' she snarled. 'Put your arms up.'

And before I had a chance to protest, she had my arms above my head, my face flat against the wall, and she proceeded to frisk me very thoroughly. I remember the days when you could call on an elderly relative and they would smile sweetly at you and give you fifty pence. Now they throw you against the nearest wall and act like Charles Bronson. Personally, I blame all these police shows on the telly.

Anyway, suffice to say this set the tone for the next few days: me, desperate to keep a low profile and stay hiding out at Gran's as long as I could, and Gran taking full advantage of the situation and ordering me about like child labour was still legal.

By the end of my second day I had done so much washing and cleaning and scrubbing that my arms were each a metre longer, and all the skin on my hands had worn off. To show you what I had to suffer, I was dragging in yet another bucketful of coal for her fire, and I thought I would offer her my advice on how having a gas fire would mean a lot less work for her than her coal fire. What did I get? I got a huge lecture on how she suffered as a child, and how hard she had had to struggle.

'You don't know the meaning of work,' she harangued me. 'When I was your age I got up every morning at half past five.'

'Why? Couldn't you sleep? I asked, all innocently.

'To go to work. Six days a week, twelve hours a day, for tuppence a day. And do you know what I would have got if I'd complained?'

I hazarded a guess: 'Four pence a day?'

'The sack,' she said.

Personally I felt that the sack seemed a better option than working all those hours, but when I suggested as much to her, she nearly jumped down my throat.

'Well that's where you're wrong!' she bellowed, 'I was one of the lucky ones.'

The lucky ones? I shuddered. Good Grief, what happened to the unlucky ones, did they boil them in oil?

'If you didn't work you didn't eat,' carried on Gran. '*And* we didn't have any shoes.'

Frankly, the connection between these two statements eluded me.

'Why?' I asked. 'Did you eat them?'

'Don't be rude!'

'I wasn't,' I protested, 'I was just—'

But Gran didn't let me finish. Grans of her sort never do.

'Do you know what I'd have got if I'd answered back?' she bellowed.

I decided it would be tactful to change the subject.

'How much do you pay for your coal?' I asked.

'A smack round the head,' bellowed Gran.

'Oh,' I said. 'That sounds cheap enough.'

The next second, Wallop! She'd hit me round the head!

Frankly I nearly left there and then, but I could not let my poor old granny down. Also The Slug was possibly still hovering around my house and the school, lying in dark corners waiting for me.

I kept in touch with what was going on in the outside world via Bernetta, who used to pop in now and then and let me know what was happening (e.g. that the Head and Wiggis had decided it was better for their mental health to let me play truant rather than set the Educational Welfare Officer on me to drag me back to school; and that there had been no sightings of The Slug).

I suppose I would have been able to hide at my Gran's for ever (or, at least, for a few weeks more), if it hadn't been for the unfortunate incident of The Washing Up.

On this particular day there seemed to be even more washing up to do than usual, and as I stood with my arms in Gran's sink and the skin on my hands turning all pink and wrinkly, I decided to make some comment.

'This is an awful lot of washing up, Gran,' I said, but gently, in case she set her false teeth on me.

'I know,' she said. 'I told my friends you'd do their washing up as well.'

I was so outraged I nearly dropped a plate. 'What?' I said.

'I don't see what you're complaining about,' said Gran. 'You wanted to help.'

'I didn't want to *help*,' I corrected her. 'I wanted to *offer* to help. The two are not the same. And also I didn't think I'd be washing up every plate ever made in the history of plate-making.'

'Don't answer back,' said Gran. 'And there's some grease still left on that plate there.'

'Where?' I said.

Gran pointed to a plate at the very bottom of the stack. Have you ever noticed that the one people want is always at the bottom of a pile?

'It looks alright to me,' I said. I nearly added: Germs have got to eat, too, but I decided it was safer not to.

'Wash it again,' said Gran.

So I did. Or, at least, I went to. The trouble was the whole pile of drying crockery must have been balanced on this one plate, because the next second the whole lot went Crash! Smack! Break! Biff! all over Gran's kitchen floor.

The result of this was that fifteen minutes later I was back home, complete with small suitcase, having narrowly beaten Gran to her front door before she could kill me and throw my remains to the birds. So ended my short period of hiding out.

I had only just got in when the front door chimes went. I assumed it was Bernetta come

to fill me in on the latest happenings at school, and tell me how the search for The Slug was going, so I trotted off to the door and opened it. It was a tactical mistake.

There on the doorstep were the two missionaries, the ex-Children of the Flowers, and it was obvious from the glares on their faces that they were intent on revenge. Quickly I tried to slam the door shut, but they had obviously built up experience from all those years of door-to-door selling their Brand of Good Works, because like lightning the one with the teeth stuck his foot in the door.

I kicked his foot to hold them up for a bit, then hurtled through the house like lightning, with the pair of them in hot pursuit.

I jerked open the back door . . . and ran straight into the arms of The Slug!!!!

11

So there I was, bouncing off the huge body of
The Slug, my whole life flashing before my eyes.
I was doomed!

Fortunately for me the two ex-missionaries
piled through the door after me, hot on my heels;
and The Slug took them to be either:
(a) my bodyguards, hired to protect me;
or
(b) plain clothes police come to arrest him.

Whatever he decided, he immediately
proceeded to set about them.

The ex-missionaries, in turn, thought The Slug
was there to protect me from them, a view
confirmed when he started beating the living
daylights out of them. They proceeded to jump
on The Slug and try to sort him out, so they
could deal with me later at their leisure.

Fortunately for me they all became so busy
with thumping each other that they temporarily
forgot about me. By the time the police put in
an appearance (screaming sirens, screeching
tyres, Miami Vice sunglasses, the lot) after being
alerted by a local nosey busy-body curious as
to what all this fighting was about (thank
heavens for nosey neighbours!), my three

would-be attackers had knocked each other out. So, as the police stormed in, with shouts of 'Freeze! Police!' and all the other sorts of police sounds they make, they found these three great hulks lying unconscious outside our back door, suffering from various forms of grievous bodily harm, and me standing over them.

Luckily for me, the Law misinterpreted the scene, and the next day the story appeared in the paper as: 'Boy Hero Beats Muggers!'

It went on to say how I had fought off three savage attackers and knocked them all unconscious. 'We say', it said, 'that this boy deserves a medal. He has given the thugs and muggers of this country a lesson they won't forget. And, who knows, with a knockout punch like this, maybe Britain has produced a World Boxing Champion of the future. Watch out, Frank Bruno!'

Wonderful stuff, eh? Dad was delighted, and spent the whole of the next day phoning up relatives and people he hadn't seen for years, just so he could say, 'By the way, did you read about our Bryan in the paper?' He proceeded to read each of them the whole story. It must have put thousands of pounds on our telephone bill.

Mum, frankly, was suspicious. She knew it had happened, the evidence was all there and the police had confirmed it, but I could tell that she felt that something was Not Right about it. Fortunately she didn't investigate too hard. The main reason for this was because she'd found a new hobby, hypnotism, and she spent most of her time going around trying to hypnotize household animals, like our cat, our goldfish, and Dad. (All, I must add, without success.)

The real stunner, though, was at school. We were in the middle of a maths lesson with Wiggis, when suddenly the door of our classroom opened and the Head breezed in and came straight towards me. For a moment my heart sank. What had he discovered about me? What sort of trouble was I in?

Instead, he stuck out his hand towards me, and said heartily, 'Boyes, allow me to shake your hand.'

Well, you could have knocked me down with a feather. From the expression on Wiggis's face, you could have knocked him down with a feather, too. However, never being one to miss an opportunity, I grabbed the Head's hand and shook it.

'Such courage,' said the Head, addressing everyone in the class. 'Such heroism. This boy is a hero. To mark the occasion, I am cancelling the scheduled maths lesson – I am sure Mr Wiggis won't object – and instead I shall ask Bryan Boyes to tell us all, in his own words, how he defeated those muggers.'

The whole class then cheered, as if he'd announced free sweets for everyone. Wiggis looked like he'd prefer to do more than object, but as the Head had announced it he just had to force a smile, and say, 'What a wonderful idea, Headmaster.'

And then, to top it all, the Head produced an autograph book and a pen, and said, 'But before you begin, may I have your autograph?'

I couldn't believe it. But that was just the start.

By the end of the day everyone at school wanted my autograph, and I was running quite a nice little number selling my autograph for ten pence. If this is fame, I thought, no wonder everyone wants to be famous!

As I walked out of school that afternoon, surrounded by my admiring fans, I reflected that life was pretty wonderful. The Slug was back behind bars. The ex-Children of the Flowers were safely out of my way. Dad thought I was wonderful. The whole world thought I was a hero. Everything was perfect, and there was nothing, absolutely nothing wrong in my life at all. Life, when all was said and done, was bliss.

Once again, I was wrong.

I had just walked out through the school gates, when a large tough-looking fellow stopped me.

'Here,' he said. 'You. You're the hero, ain't you? The kid what knocked out three attackers single-handed.'

Another admirer, I thought. Aloud I said modestly, 'I cannot deny it. I suppose you want my autograph?'

'No,' he growled. 'I wanna fight you.'

I was shocked. Fight me? For one awful moment I thought he might have been a relative of The Slug's, but he looked too human.

'Come on,' he said, holding up his fists, all ready to fight. 'Put 'em up.'

'Are you mad?' I said, determined to talk him out of forcing me into a punch-up. 'Don't you read the papers? I'm a killing machine.' And I showed him my fists (which, truth to tell, didn't look nearly as big as his). 'These fists have knocked out three people with one punch.'

'I know,' he said. 'So come on, I wanna fight you.'

Faced with such an out-and-out kamikaze maniac as this, I was stuck. There was only one answer: sneer my way out. I curled my lip into a contemptuous smile, and then said, 'Of course you would, wouldn't you, knowing that I'm at a temporary disadvantage because my fists are damaged?'

This had him, I could tell by the baffled look on his face.

'Eh? What do you mean?'

'From knocking out those three attackers. But of course, if you can only pick on disabled people—'

It did the trick.

'Well,' he said uncomfortably, 'I didn't know—'

Then I delivered the *coup de grâce* (after all, I was surrounded by my admiring fans and I didn't want them to think that Their New Hero was backing down from a fight).

'But', I snapped, 'when my hand is better, I will meet you at any place you choose. And beat you.'

And with that I swept off, with the cheers of my fans ringing in my ears, and my would-be opponent slinking away with his tail between his legs. However, it had been a very close call.

It wasn't long before I discovered that this was to be no isolated incident. Within the next three days no less than seven people came up and challenged me to a fight. Seven! Honestly, I

couldn't understand the mentality of these lunatics. I mean, if I knew that someone could knock three people out in one go, would I go out of my way to pick a fight with them? Absolutely not. No way. I even went into a shop for an ice-cream and some horrible little kid of about five challenged me to a fight. As he was smaller than me I trod on his cornet, but it was symptomatic of a whole new plague in my life.

I did my best to talk my way out of all these challenges, which used up a lot of brainpower, and generally I was successful. Successful, that is, until one fateful day when this huge lumbering idiot called Potter, who thinks he's the Rocky VI of our school, cornered me in the playground.

As always I was surrounded by my admirers (I kept them contented by signing my autograph for them every break-time). I had taken the precaution of making sure that I spent every break-time leaning against a wall just underneath the Headmaster's window. This usually frightened people off challenging me to a fight, because they knew that the Head would hear, and they would get into trouble. It would also mean that any such fight would be stopped by the Head. That, at least, was my theory.

On this particular day I saw Potter making his way towards me, and knew that yet another gauntlet was going to be thrown down. I shot a quick look at the Head's window and was reassured to see him in there, even if he was on the phone.

As I expected, Potter, being completely unsubtle, came straight out with his challenge.

He pushed his way through the ranks of my admirers, put his fists up, and snapped, 'Alright, hero! Come and fight!'

I looked round at my admirers as they waited expectantly for my reaction, then curled my lip in my now well-known contemptuous sneer and said loudly, 'You want to fight *me*?!'

'Yes,' said Potter.

'Ha!' I said scornfully, and cast another quick look at the Head's window, waiting for him to intervene. Unfortunately he was still on the telephone, which was a bit of a nuisance. So a little bit louder this time, I barked at Potter, 'When do you want to FIGHT ME?'

'Now,' said Potter, and then he added, puzzled, 'What are you shouting for?'

I didn't like the way this was going. I curled my lip a little more, which meant it was now almost a third nostril, and said in an even louder voice, full of contempt, to my admirers, 'Did you hear that? HE WANTS TO FIGHT ME NOW!'

I was starting to sweat slightly now, and was just thinking, maybe the Head had gone deaf, in which case I was in serious trouble, when luckily the window above us opened and the Head looked out.

'What's going on?' he demanded.

As always happens in cases like this, everyone fell silent.

'Well?' demanded the Head.

I was just wondering if I was going to have to lose face and blurt out the story, when Weed did it for me instead, which gave me an excuse to look at him with contempt in my eyes as a squealer.

'Potter challenged Boyes to a fight, sir,' said Weed.

'But I would not take him up on it, sir,' I said, full of heroism and sportsmanship. 'Not because I am afraid, but because I honour the name of the school too much to sully it by brawling in the playground. Even though I could beat Potter with both hands tied behind my back.'

At this there was some whispered cheering from my admirers, but not too loud because the Head was still halfway out of his window and looking down on us. The Head, however, was impressed by my little speech. He smiled approvingly and said, 'Admirable sentiments, Boyes. Well done.'

I was just patting myself mentally on the back when Potter, eager not to be outdone, snorted, 'Nah. The reason he won't fight is because he's a coward.'

Well this was too much for my admirers, who started muttering in shocked tones, and murmuring things like 'Show him, Bryan.' It was obvious to me that I had to do something quick, so I yelled, 'A coward?! Hold me back before I beat him to a pulp.'

Then I grabbed Weed's arm and held it across my chest to 'stop me', while the Head intervened, as I'd hoped he would.

'Boys, boys—' he said.

'But I have been called a coward, sir,' I protested, keen to make sure that I saved my reputation as a hero without having to fight for it.

'I understand your dilemma, Boyes,' said the

Head sympathetically. 'But I will not tolerate brawling in this school.'

Thank heavens for that, I thought.

'However,' continued the Head, 'I think in this case we can come to an arrangement.'

A shiver of fear ran up and down my spine.

'An arrangement?' I said.

'Yes,' said the Head. 'I suggest we hold a properly refereed boxing match. It is some years since we had boxing at this school, but in these circumstances I think we can justify it. After all, it is a matter of honour.'

And with that all my stupid, idiotic, cretinous admirers started cheering, and Potter called for three cheers for the Head. And all I wanted to do was fall down and faint. Me? Box? Aaaargh!!!

12

It seemed to me that there was only one way to get out of this boxing match (and get out of it I had to for two reasons: (a) because if I didn't Potter would beat me to a pulp; and (b) that would prove that the whole business of me being a hero was a fake, and then everyone else would want to thump me, too, for having taken them for a ride). The way out was to use the influence of my parents. Mum is notoriously anti-boxing. Whenever it appears on the television she immediately switches it over to another channel, and then gives Dad and me a huge lecture about how insane, obscene, etc., it is. Without doubt, Mum would put her foot down and make sure this ritual execution did not go ahead.

Luckily for me, Mum had decided to give me her attention that evening. Not because she thought I deserved it, but because she wanted to use me as her latest guinea pig in her experiments with hypnotism. She sat me in an armchair, and dangled her necklace in front of my eyes, murmuring things like, 'Listen to my voice,' and 'You are feeling sleepy.' Actually with the fear of being bashed to smithereens by Potter, nothing on earth could have made me feel sleepy, let alone hypnotism.

'Do you want to know what happened to me at school today?' I asked, after a suitable length of time watching her necklace swinging from side to side.

'Shut up,' said Mum. 'Concentrate.'

I concentrated.

'How long do I have to concentrate for?' I asked after what seemed like ten light years.

Mum got up in disgust.

'You're a waste of time,' she said. 'Both of you.'

Dad's ears turned pink as he worked on his crossword and pretended not to hear her.

'Neither of you are interested in helping me with this at all.'

And with that she went over to the fishtank and started swinging the necklace in front of our goldfish. I decided to attack this boxing problem from another angle, working on Mum via Dad, which nearly always works.

'Dad?' I said.

'Yes?' said Dad, popping up from his newspaper.

'Don't you think that boxing is cruel and disgusting?'

'Boxing?' said Dad, 'Well – er—'

'It is barbaric,' snorted Mum, just as I'd hoped. 'Two men beating each other up for other people's entertainment. It is sickening.'

'Absolutely,' nodded Dad in agreement.

This was what I wanted.

'It's as bad as bear-baiting,' threw in Dad, just to let Mum know he was on her side.

'It ought to be banned completely and absolutely,' said Mum.

'Absolutely,' echoed Dad, just in case we hadn't heard him the first time.

Good, now was the time to throw in my news.

'Our Headmaster's fixed up a boxing match for me,' I said.

The expressions on Mum's and Dad's faces were a sight for sore eyes, a perfect vision for me with the threat of Potter hanging over my head.

'What?!' they said in unison.

I nodded.

'So if you want to phone him and insist that it's cancelled, I'll understand.'

For some reason, they didn't rush to the phone.

'Well. . . ,' said Mum, a bit too hesitantly, I thought. I decided to push the matter on a bit while she was still in a hot rage about boxing as a blood sport.

'If you want to phone him at home, his number is 675—' I began.

'I don't think we ought to be too hasty,' said Mum slowly.

A nasty cold chill went up and down my spine. This chill was starting to run up and down it so often lately I wondered if I was going to catch a cold in my back.

'Why not?' I asked.

'Well,' said Mum, 'at some levels it is still a sport.'

'And it does seem like a sport that you are good at,' added Dad. 'Remember what the paper said about your punch: 'Watch out, Frank Bruno!''

I was outraged! The hyprocrites!

'A minute ago you were saying that it ought to be banned!' I pointed out in some anger.

'Yes,' said Mum, 'but if it's something that you really want to do it would be unfair of us to stand in your way.'

'And you could become famous at it,' said Dad.

'But this kid wants to beat me up, just because I'm a hero!'

'That's always the way,' said Dad. 'Get a reputation as the best and everyone wants to beat you. The same happened to me when I was your age. I was Dominoes Champion at my youth club.'

'Dominoes? They don't punch your head in with a domino!' I pointed out.

'Your father's right,' said Mum. 'And if it's going to happen, it's better that it happens in the proper circumstances rather than in some back street.'

And with that she went back to trying to hypnotize some sea-weed in the fish-tank. I just sat their, dumbstruck. Sunk by my own parents! What price their principles, that was what I wanted to know!

The next day at school things took a turn for the even worse. I was lounging around in the corridor with Bernetta, both of us trying to work out a strategy by which I could be injured (without too much injury) just before the fight, and so not have to fight but also not lose face, when who should come along but Juggs and Wally. Juggs and Wally are two of the school's toughest Fifth Years, and are also the school bookies. From the way they settled in alongside me and Bernetta, it was obvious that they

wanted to discuss something with us. I knew I didn't owe them any money because it is a point of principle with me never to bet, mainly because if you lose you can't pay, then people jump up and down on you with big boots on, which is not a healthy activity for the person being jumped on. Perhaps it was Bernetta they wanted to see. Wally's opening line proved that was not the case.

'We'd like a word wiv the 'ero 'ere,' he said. 'So run along, darlin'.'

Bernetta looked at me, unsure as to what to do? Should she run along, or what?

I put on an air of bravado and said, 'I'd watch the way I talked if I were you. Remember, I knocked out three people single-handed.'

For some reason Wally and Juggs exchanged amused glances at this, which I didn't like. Then Wally (who usually did most of the talking for both of them) said, 'Well we know there's only two of us, but we're willing to give it a go.'

This seemed to me to be moving on to dangerous ground. I turned to Bernetta, and, forcing a nonchalant tone of voice, said airily, 'Everyone wants to challenge me. You'd better run along, Bernetta, this could mean bloodshed and I don't want to upset you. I'll see you later.'

Bernetta hesitated a moment, though I wasn't sure why. Me, I sould have been off down the corridor like a rocket as soon as I realized Juggs and Wally were in the offing. However, after a second's pause, Bernetta moved off. I then turned my attention to the school's own Ladbrokes, still keeping up my air of The Hero.

'Lucky I didn't take you seriously there,' I said. 'You could have been in serious trouble. Remember what happened to The Slug.'

Again, Wally and Juggs exchanged these grins, and Wally said: 'Funny you should mention that,' in the sort of voice that made me think that this wasn't going to be funny for me at all.

'Oh?' I said cautiously.

'Because Juggs here knows someone.'

'Oh?' I said again.

'And that someone knows someone who knows someone who knows someone.'

'He knows a lot of people,' I commented.

'And,' added Wally with a sly grin, 'one of those someones just happens to work in the nick where they took The Slug after he was picked up at your place. And he tells a very different story about who knocked out who. If you get my meaning.'

I got his meaning alright, but I decided to keep up my act for as long as I could. My health was at stake here.

'I expect he was delirious,' I said. 'The strength of my punch possibly turned his brain.'

'Maybe,' said Wally, 'or maybe this Big Fight you and Potter are having is not gonna turn out the way everyone thinks.'

He let this sink in. I tried to let it sink in, but I couldn't quite work out what he was getting at. He made it clearer.

'As you know, we run the book in this school, and at the moment everyone reckons you're the hot shot, so all their money's going on you. Therefore if you win, we stand to lose a lot of money.'

I could suddenly see where this conversation was heading.

'Now it could be this story we heard is not true, and you really can take on three people and beat them. In which case, if you win on Thursday, we're gonna have to send *four* people round to talk to you very severely. On the other hand, you might just lose naturally. Which would be better for your health.'

I said nothing. Frankly there wasn't a lot I could say, except a very frightened 'Help!' and I couldn't do that because I was supposed to be A Hero. All I could do was lean against the wall (which helped to stop me falling over in fear) and pass it off with as much bravado as I could. Fortunately Juggs and Wally had decided that they'd given me their party political broadcast, and could now wander off.

Phew! I groaned to myself as they started to amble off. It seemed to me that there was only one answer. I would have to go sick on the night of the fight and not turn up.

That thought vanished with Wally's final words, as they reached the end of the corridor.

'By the way,' he called back. 'Don't think about not turning up. We'd hate for all bets to be null and void.'

And with that they went, and I slid to the floor and tried to recover my fast vanishing self-confidence.

Still, as I have said before, we dodgers are at our best when everything seems at its worst for us, and such was the case here. In fact, maybe Juggs and Wally had given me the perfect ammunition I needed to get this whole boxing match fiasco cancelled and forgotten about. With that thought in mind I made straight for the Headmaster's office.

'Sir,' I said. 'I have some grave news for you.'

'Ah, Boyes,' he said when he had come down from the ceiling, because I had obviously frightened him by the speed of my entry into his office. 'Not too grave, I hope. How's the training going?'

'Training?'

'For the boxing match. Only two days to go, you know.'

I put on my This Is Very Serious look, and said, 'That's what I want to talk to you about, sir.'

'Oh?'

'Far be it from me to tell tales on my schoolmates.'

'Er, absolutely,' agreed the Head, taken aback.

'I believe,' I continued, warming to my theme, 'that loyalty to one's schoolmates ranks alongside honesty, patriotism and respect for one's parents as the virtues that have made this country what it is today.'

Strong stuff, eh? It's the sort of stuff that when you hear it on the telly it's usually followed by the person who said it announcing Vote For Me. The Head just looked at me, baffled.

'Er, yes,' he said.

'But the good name of this school, sir, is being sullied.'

'Sullied?'

'It pains me to tell you this, but certain Fifth Years are running a betting book on the outcome of this match.'

'Are they?' said the Head. 'Oh dear.'

It wasn't quite the reaction I had hoped for. I'd have preferred a bit more anger and outrage, but it would do for starters.

'Because of this,' I continued, 'I will understand if you decide to cancel it.'

'Cancel it?'

'I understand.' And before he had a chance to change his mind, I headed towards the door, saying, 'I'll get it cancelled right away.'

'Wait!' yelped the Head.

I stopped.

'Sir?' I said.

'Why should it be cancelled?' said the Head, obviously still none the wiser as to what my visit had been about.

'Because it has been tainted by this gambling,' I said.

At last it sank in.

'You mean that you would sacrifice this chance to defend your honour, on a point of principle?' he said, amazed and impressed.

'I would, sir,' I said bravely.

For a minute I thought I had him, but then: 'No,' he said. 'No, I cannot let you do it. I know what this contest means to you, Boyes. Your honour has been called into question.'

'I can live with that, sir,' I said desperately.

'As for this gambling, I'm sure it isn't serious. It's not as if anyone's going to get hurt because of it.' And here he even had the nerve to give a light laugh. Not get hurt because of it! To say that to me, who was at risk of getting hurt from any one of a dozen different directions because

of it! 'It could even improve the maths in the school.'

'But—' I began.

I was out of luck. He got up and opened the door, with these dreaded words putting the final nail in my coffin, 'There's no need to thank me, Boyes. I only wish I could be in your place.'

And with that I found myself outside in the corridor, doomed.

I spent the whole of the next two days trying everything I could think of to get out of climbing into that ring with that homicidal maniac, Potter, without openly admitting that I was not really A Hero.

I tried pretending to be ill. I told my Mum that I had a headache and double vision, that my stomach was in agony, and I had pains in both legs and both arms. All she said was: 'Pretending again, huh?' and forced me to go to school.

I tried to pretend that I'd been run over, but every time I ventured out to poise myself on the edge of the pavement all ready for my alibi, someone came up and started talking to me about The Big Fight, and how they wished they were me.

So it was that Thursday afternoon found me trapped in the changing room at our school, dressed in boxing shorts and wearing a pair of boxing gloves that were bigger than anything I'd ever seen. It looked like I had a bowling ball stuck on the end of each arm. It did cross my mind that maybe I could swap them for a bowling ball each, but the trouble was I wouldn't be able to lift them to hit Potter. Also, people would notice.

It was all so tragically ironic. I had defeated The Slug, I had defeated the two missionaries from the Children of the Flowers. I had defeated Wiggis. I had defeated the Worples (well, almost) and all the other pet owners who wanted to do me damage. All of those people I had got away from without one hair of my head being harmed (unless you counted the hair that Gran thumped). All that success, and eluding the opposition so brilliantly, so cleverly, so skilfully, yet to come to this! To be trapped into being thumped into pudding and in front of everybody, and with everyone giving their permission for me being thumped! And them thinking I was going to enjoy it! It was tragic. There seemed to be no way out for me this time. Yet there had to be a way!

It was as these thoughts were turning round in my brain that the door to the changing room opened and Dad and Mum came in. Dad had taken the afternoon off work, so keen was he to see me get slaughtered, and Mum had obviously suspended her anti-boxing feelings for the afternoon.

'Hello, Champ,' grinned Dad. 'We thought we'd pop in and let you know you won't be alone in that ring.'

'I know,' I groaned miserably; 'there'll be another bloke in there trying to hit me.'

Dad just laughed at this, sure that I was making a joke. As if any normal human being would joke at a time like this!

'We'll be beside you,' he said in what was meant to be a reassuring voice.

'Couldn't you be in front of me?'

Again he laughed that stupid braying laugh, then he and Mum went off to find their seats for the killing. I just sat there and sank further and further into gloom. Was this how Frank Bruno felt before every fight? I asked myself. If so, why didn't he pack it in?

I groaned aloud, and as I did so the door opened and Bernetta came in.

'Are you alright?' she asked.

'Of course I'm not alright,' I said. 'I've got to go out there and get killed. Would you be alright if that fate was facing you?'

'I just thought I'd pop in to see if I could help.'

'You can fight Potter for me,' I suggested.

After all, with a bit of a disguise . . . but no, it wasn't fair, even if it was safer for me.

'Have you thought of bribing him?' she suggested.

'He doesn't want to be bribed, all he wants to do is hit me,' I groaned. Suddenly an idea hit me: 'I know!'

'What?'

'Just as the fight is about to start, you sound the fire alarm.'

'I thought of that,' she said, 'but it won't work.'

'Why not?' I asked.

'All they'll do is have the fight another time.'

'You're right,' I groaned again. I might have known that someone as astute as Bernetta would have thought of that one and seen the flaws. Then another idea hit me. It shows how desperate I was, my brain was clutching at any straw that came to it.

'You can still get me out of this, though.'

'How?'

'Go and tell Potter that I'm seriously ill. Tell him I've got a bad heart, or something.'

'What good will that do?'

'It might make him feel sorry for me and stop him hitting me. Tell him I'm an orphan as well.'

'I can't see it working.'

'It's worth a try. It's the only chance I've got of coming back here with all my bits and pieces still in the same place.'

So off she went. She was back within minutes, and by the expression on her face her mission had not been a success.

'Well?' I asked her, even though I knew the answer. 'What did he say?'

'He's going to punch your head in.'

And with those words my last hope went.

'You must have said it all wrong, I said accusingly. 'Are you sure you told him I'm an orphan?'

'Yes, but it didn't do much good,' she said. 'Your Mum went in to see him straight after I left him.'

The traitress! How could she? Hob-nobbing with the thug who was going to punch her precious son's nose through the back of his head. I was betrayed!

'Right,' I said determinedly, 'that settles it.'

And with that I started hauling my clothes out of the locker, a difficult job with huge boxing gloves on, but these were difficult times.

'What are you going to do?' asked Bernetta.

'The only sensible thing,' I said. 'I'm going to make a run for it.'

I was out of luck. The next second the door of the changing room opened and Wiggis and the Senior Science Teacher appeared. Wiggis had offered (to gratify his sadistic leanings) to act as my second, and now here he was ready to make sure I received all the punishment he had wanted to hand out to me himself.

'Well, Boyes,' he grinned gleefully, 'they're all ready for you out there.'

I tried my last throw. I tried to resurrect my 'loss of memory' con.

'There's been a mistake,' I protested. 'Who are you? What is this place? Where am I?'

Wiggis was the wrong person to try that one on. Without another word he leapt upon me, and I found myself being dragged out of the changing room and off towards the school hall, where the torture chamber known as the boxing ring had been set up, my heels digging deep furrows in the floor of the corridor as we went. I wasn't giving up without one last struggle. But it was all no use.

Five minutes later I was sitting on a stool in the make-shift boxing ring, the eyes of the whole school upon me. In the other corner of the ring sat Potter, now looking about ten feet tall, and with muscles in places where I haven't even got places. This wasn't going to be a fight, this was going to be a massacre. My only chance was to walk to the centre of the ring, and then collapse in a 'faint' before he could hit me, and claim later that I had been overcome by the heat. One thing was certain, I daren't let Potter get within two metres of me or my head would be repositioned somewhere around my boxing shorts.

I looked at the ringside seats. There were my Dad and Mum, both smiling at me. The smile my Mum gave me was the worst, because she actually looked so confident. Did she really want me bashed up that much? Her poor son? Her poor boy whom she had dandled on her knee when he was a baby?

The Headmaster was acting as Master of Ceremonies for the occasion, and as he got into the ring I started to pray that he was going to make one of his long speeches, the sort that he makes at the start of a new term. They always take about half an hour, and with a bit of luck by that time Potter would have forgotten what he was there for.

No such luck. The Head just announced the fight, introduced the referee, announced me and Potter to the crowd (as if they didn't already know who we were), and then stepped out of the ring. So much for wishing he could be in my place! The next second there was the ominous Dong! of a bell announcing the start of Round One.

I got up, just about, although I thought for a minute my legs weren't even going to make it to the centre of the ring, where I could collapse dramatically. I took one step forward. Potter got up, and then he fell over. And he stayed fallen over.

I was stunned. What had happened? The crowd went berserk, calling for him to get up. The referee looked at the Head, who just looked back at him as baffled as everyone else. So then the referee did the only thing he could do, he counted to ten over the fallen figure of Potter, who just lay there flat out with his eyes closed and a stupid

sort of smile on his face. Then the referee walked over to me, held my hand up, and announced me as The Winner!

There was pandemonium, with everyone jumping up and down and cheering and yelling, and shouting out 'Boyes is The Champ! Boyes is The Champ!' In the middle of all this uproar, Potter woke up, lurched to his feet, and looked blankly about him. When he realized what had happened he got all angry and wanted to start the fight again, but it was too late, it was over. I was still puzzled. Looking at Potter, the way he had acted then and the way he was acting now, it was almost as if he was coming out of a hypnotic trance.

A hypnotic trance? I shot a quick glance at Mum, who now smiled back and waved her necklace at me. No, surely it wasn't possible? But Bernetta had seen her going into Potter's changing room just before the fight. . . .

No, it wasn't possible! Or was it?

Again I stole a quick glance at Mum, but now she was talking to Dad, and Bernetta and the Head were both shaking me by the boxing gloves and telling me how wonderful I was. So, I guess we will never know what happened to Potter. All I do know is the answer to the question: What happened to Boyes? I survived. And that, I think, is a pretty wonderful thing to happen.